CHARLESTON
ON THE
POTOMAC

The Roaring Twenties Trilogy

Charleston's Lonely Heart Hotel
Charleston's House of Stuart
Charleston on the Potomac

CHARLESTON
ON THE
POTOMAC

Steve Brown

CHICK SPRINGS
PUBLISHING™
SOUTH
CAROLINA

Author's Note

This is a work of fiction. Names, characters, places, and incidents are products of the author's imagination or are used fictitiously. Any resemblance to actual events, specific locales, organizations, or persons, living or dead, is entirely coincidental and beyond the intent of either the author or the publisher.

Acknowledgments

For their assistance in preparing this story, I would like to thank Mark Brown, Sonya Caldwell, Sally Heineman, Missy Johnson, Cindy Johnson, Stacey King, Kate Lehman, Jean Lewis, Susan Snowden, Helen Turnage, Ellis Vidler, Dwight Watt, and, of course, Mary Ella.

For Wally Mullinax and my cousins, Jean Lewis and Betty Swift, two more enthusiastic yellow-dog Democrats you could never find.

The House of Stuart:

James	husband
Hartleigh	his wife
Sue Ellen	his sister
Cousin Katie	from Greenville
Tessa	James's niece
Dory Campbell	runaway
Eileen	James's mother
Elizabeth Randolph	James's mother-in-law
Lee Randolph	Virginian

The Belles of Charleston:

Rachel	wife of Christian Andersen
Christian	formerly of Dairyland, Wisconsin
Georgiana	Rachel's stepmother
Lewis Belle	Stuart family attorney
Nell	Rachel's sister-in-law

Others:

Jim Byrnes	former Third District congressman
Prescott Mitchell	Stuart warehouse manager
Royce Craven	land-poor Charlestonian
Billy Ray Craven	his son, assistant county solicitor
Susan Moultrie	the former Susan Chase
Whitney	Stuart and Company accountant

The Help:

Alexander	manservant
Pearl	his wife, the Stuarts' cook
Molly	her sister

When Jim Byrnes concluded his business in Washington, for every dollar South Carolina sent to the federal treasury, twenty-seven dollars were returned to the state of South Carolina.

— James Stuart

ONE

1930

"James, you favor one twin over the other and your daughter probably worships you more than your son."

No response from her husband.

His wife glanced at the parlor door, then raised her voice. "James!"

Her husband, in the companion wingback chair, lowered his newspaper. "Pardon?" James Stuart had an incredible talent for concentration and occasionally that worked to his disadvantage.

Hartleigh repeated her accusation at the same time that her mother strolled into the parlor.

As James rose to his feet, Elizabeth Randolph said, "Just remember, James, Hartleigh has your best interest at heart."

"Mother!" Her daughter's hand rose to her throat. "I thought you'd gone to bed."

"Just waiting for Dory to come in." She glanced at the parlor door. "It doesn't take that much time to see someone off from Union Station."

Elegantly dressed in the latest fashion from Paris—all handmade dresses and gowns; none of that ready-to-wear and off-the-rack styling for her— Elizabeth Randolph took a seat on the love seat next to a needlepoint canvas she was working on. She'd recently returned from a grand tour of Europe only to learn she'd lost everything in the crash of 1929.

"As your wife says, you favor your son over Mary Anne." She had small, prim features and gray hair swept up in an old-fashioned bun.

James returned to his seat. Truth be known, he was uncomfortable handling his daughter. Mary Anne felt so fragile and breakable. He really didn't know what to do with her.

While her mother brushed down the hem of her dress, Hartleigh flashed a nervous smile at her husband.

James was a tall, lanky man with ropy muscles who wore three-piece suits, usually with a regimental tie. James had served in the Great War, and his wife was pleased that he no longer sported a military haircut but had allowed his hair to lengthen so it could be plastered down, keeping it neatly in place.

He cleared his throat. "What do you suggest?"

"When you go in to see the twins after they've said their prayers, you might kiss Mary Anne first, then young James. That would be a good habit to get into."

"You mean favor one child over the other?"

"Rather, in this case," said his mother-in-law with ice in her voice, "you could explain that ladies go first."

James considered her suggestion. "I'll see what I can do." And he returned to his newspaper.

But Elizabeth was not through. "And it wouldn't hurt if you read them a story from time to time."

"Mother, please," pleaded Hartleigh. Next, her mother would suggest that her husband change a diaper or two.

The phone in the hallway rang, and the butler answered it. Moments later, he appeared at the parlor door.

"It's for you, Mister James." In the South if you were a black man and you reached the age of forty, you were like a rock. The butler was such a Negro.

When James stood, he nodded to his mother-in-law. "With your permission, madam." James steadfastly refused to address his mother-in-law as "Mother."

"Of course." Elizabeth glanced at her wristwatch. "Whoever it is ask them not to call this late again. It's after eight."

"Yes, ma'am."

On the other end of the line of a phone on a table in the downstairs hallway was Jimmy Byrnes, a former congressman who six years earlier had made a run for the United States Senate. In that race, Byrnes had narrowly lost.

"Yes, Congressman, what can I do for you?"

"Are you on your hall phone or the one in your study?"

"The one in the hall."

"Would you give me the other number so the operator can place a call? Your friends didn't have that number."

"What friends?"

"Turner Logan." Turner Logan had hired James to be the site engineer for building the first bridge over the Cooper River.

James gave Byrnes the number, hung up, and returned to the parlor. "Please excuse me, but I need to take this call."

"Really, James," said his mother-in-law, "it's rather late to be talking on the telephone. You're not some teenager."

"Yes, ma'am, and I hope you'll excuse me." After a slight bow, James left the parlor for the stairs.

"That telephone," muttered Elizabeth. "People call at all hours and about the most trivial matters."

Upstairs, James knocked on one of the bedroom doors. Wearing a crimson and gold robe, Christian Andersen opened the door. James thought the robe was the ugliest garment ever worn by man and could've been purchased only by a wife.

"Could you join me in the study?" he asked. "There's a phone call coming through."

Christian turned to his wife. The young couple had been reading in bed; he, the latest issue of *Popular Mechanics*; she, *The Old Clock*, and though the detective was still in high school, Rachel had been immediately drawn into the story. In the background, the orchestra on the radio was being fronted by Harry Richman performing "Puttin' on the Ritz," and baby Jonathan slept in a bassinette on his mother's side of the bed. Christian and Rachel were bunking with the Stuarts while their home on High Battery was being renovated. Without looking up, Rachel waved her husband away. Nancy Drew had finally secured the old clock.

Leaving his robe behind and pulling on a dress shirt, Christian followed James downstairs. During their descent, James explained that Jim Byrnes had been turned out of office when he left the House of Representatives to run against Coley Blease, a former governor. In his corner, Byrnes had the farmers and

the progressives while Coley Blease had the support
of the textile workers. Fifty years ago textile workers
had been an insignificant voting bloc, but now there
were over seventy thousand in the state, and most
of them would vote for anyone who promised to keep
the Negro out of the body politic, and especially the
labor pool.

This time, Byrnes had a much better chance to
unseat Blease. Coley Blease represented the good
times of the previous decade while Jimmy Byrnes
promised to roll up his sleeves and go to work in
Washington to pull the country out of the worst
recession since the crash of '93. Still, it would be
difficult to defeat a sitting senator, and that's why
Byrnes had called James.

Hearing the two young men turn in the direction
of the study, Elizabeth Randolph looked up from her
needlepoint. "How much longer will the Andersens
be living here?"

"As long as they like, Mother. They don't want the
baby breathing all that plaster dust."

"Well, they could live down the street at the Belle
mansion."

"This is my husband's house, and I don't think
it's my place to send people packing. No telling where
that might lead."

In the study, Christian poured each of them a shot
of brandy. Born and raised in Dairyland, Wisconsin,
Christian had been educated at the University of
Chicago, then came south to participate in building
the bridge over the Cooper River. He'd done such
a fine job that by the end of the project he'd been
put in charge of the East Cooper side and won the
confidence of James Stuart. Along the way, Christian
had also won the heart of Rachel Belle, who defied her

father by marrying a Yankee. Their son, Jonathan, was a combination of their genetic pools with blond hair from Christian's family and crystal-clear blue eyes and pale skin from his mother's.

When the phone rang, Christian reached across the desk and flipped a switch, then placed the handset in its cradle.

James lit a cheroot and let out a breath. "I asked my partner, Christian Andersen, to sit in. I have one of those new Ericsson group phones, and you might hear a bit of feedback, but it keeps Christian and me from having to go head-to-head with the receiver between our ears."

"A group phone?" asked Byrnes from his law office in Spartanburg. "What will they think of next? Anyway, phone calls are expensive so let's get down to brass tacks. You may remember that when Coley Blease and I ran against each other six years ago Coley called me a Catholic, even though I'd become an Episcopalian when I married Maude. And then, before the primary, a letter was released to the newspapers from twenty good Catholics who swore they'd served with me as an altar boy but felt I would still make an excellent senator."

James recalled the day the letter had been made public; he had commented to Lewis Belle, the Stuart family attorney, that Jim Byrnes's political goose was cooked. Few Catholics were ever elected to public office in the South, or, for that matter, anywhere else in the country. Lewis was a frustrated politician in his own right. He refused to pander to the masses, and on that particular day, he had become all worked up about what he termed a "dirty trick." The letter resulted in Byrnes's political enemies being able to say that if Jimmy Byrnes were elected, the Pope would have his own senator from the state of South Carolina.

STEVE BROWN

In the one-party rule of the American South, all a candidate had to do was win the Democratic primary. Republicans did not nominate candidates in the Deep South, and over the years, Washington lobbyists had learned that American presidents might come and go, but members of Congress from the Deep South usually died in office.

"I'm going to beat Coley because Coley Blease is wrong for the times. Maude and I have traveled the state, and the devastation we've seen from this state's dependency on cotton is beyond belief. I found only three cotton mills in full production, and people's wages must come from somewhere. It certainly won't be cotton. Cotton may go as low as a nickel a pound."

"A nickel?" Christian had grown up on a dairy farm and knew the disaster that could be wrought with a one-crop farm; in his family's case, milk.

"Yes, Mister Andersen, if prices continue to fall."

"It's 'Christian.' Mister Andersen is my father."

"And I'm 'Jim.' Captain Stuart, I can't match Coley's rhetoric on the stump, but I can match him on the radio. When Coley feels the heat, he's going to start racing around the state making more and more stump speeches, but I'll match him with commercial time on the radio. Radio's the new stump, but Coley doesn't understand that. Still, and this is why I called, it would be good if there were another candidate in the senate race. Coley is at his most vulnerable in a runoff."

Christian Andersen smiled.

"What are you grinning about?" asked James. "If I assist the congressman, you'll be responsible for Stuart and Company."

"I'd be more enthused about his prospects if the company bore my name."

From Spartanburg came Byrnes's laugh. "Now there's a real Yankee trader if I've ever heard one."

7

"Are you saying the business should be called Andersen and Company?" asked James.

"Of course not. I'm still a damn Yankee." Yankees returned up north. Damn Yankees remained in the South.

"So the company's name should be Stuart and Andersen."

"Well," said Christian with a grin, "I'm not averse to the business being called Andersen and Stuart. After all, it's alphabetically correct."

Another laugh from Spartanburg, and James told the former congressman he'd see what he could do.

After the call, Christian asked, "Tell me, James, is working for a politician a step up or a step down from being a bootlegger?"

TWO

Christian left James smoking one of his cherished cheroots and plotting. It was going to be a long night for James, but a fun night for Christian. At the top of the stairs, Christian did a little jig outside his bedroom door, waving around a bottle of sherry he'd confiscated from the study's wet bar.

Put down your murder mystery, my dear, your husband has been promoted and we're going to celebrate.

But as he reached for the bedroom door, a commotion erupted below him. Christian looked over the railing and saw the butler opening the front door and two teenage girls stumbling inside. The girls were quickly followed by a young man who cut a dashing figure in his fashionable clothing. All three disappeared into the parlor.

Over the years, Christian had learned that

Charleston was inhabited by some rather extraordinary characters who loved to gossip, so, handing off the bottle of sherry to the upstairs maid, Christian drifted back downstairs.

In the parlor, Dory Campbell said, "Look who we found at the train station when we were seeing off the Grimke sisters."

Dory Campbell was a runaway who had been taken in by Elizabeth Randolph. At the time, Dory was a skinny country girl with curly brown hair, freckles, and an unsure manner, but after a year at a girls' prep school in New England and a grand tour of Europe, Dory had become a confident young woman with only the occasional thought that the rug might suddenly be pulled out from under her.

Dory's companion, Tessa Stuart, was a twelfth generation Charlestonian who lived next door with her grandmother. Because her mother had died from infantile paralysis and her father was often at sea, Tessa spent much of her time in this house, especially after Dory returned from her grand tour.

Tessa had reddish-brown hair and a curvaceous body, and since the flapper era had succumbed to the stark economic realities of the day, she wore fairly conservative clothing. In the space of a single season, the tomboy dress, as it was called in France, disappeared in a fog of conventionality, and women began to wear longer skirts with waistlines returning to their normal position. The cloche hat and bobbed hair remained, but Tessa's generation no longer wrapped their curves in an attempt to create a boyish figure.

Elizabeth Randolph believed Tessa Stuart to be a bad influence on Dory, but Hartleigh knew it to be vice versa.

The young man was Lee Randolph, a Virginia

cousin of Elizabeth and Hartleigh. Lee had good shoulders, a sly smile, and a thin mustache; he wore a double-breasted vest with a single-breasted coat and baggy trousers. Under his hat was a thatch of curly brown hair. He handed his fedora to the butler and bowed to Elizabeth and Hartleigh, then leaned down and pecked each of them on the cheek.

"Why, Lee," said Elizabeth, putting down her needlepoint, "you're early. We weren't expecting you until next week."

"Yes, and I hope you have room for me."

"Certainly." Elizabeth took a small silver bell from the end table and rang it.

The butler reappeared at the parlor door. "Yes, ma'am."

"Master Randolph has arrived early. Can you see to his accommodations?"

"Of course, madam."

Elizabeth returned her attention to the Virginian. "Give them a few minutes."

"Very well," said Lee. "It would appear that a year abroad agreed with you."

"Thank you."

To Hartleigh, Lee said, "I haven't seen you since the wedding. Hope that bootlegger's treating you well."

Hartleigh flashed a phony smile. She resented those who denigrated her husband's work, especially since so many important families were doing so poorly, such as the Randolphs of Virginia. "Thank you, Lee. The twins will be a year old by Memorial Day."

Lee went to stand in front of a dormant fireplace. While his back was turned, Elizabeth flashed an I-told-you-so look at her daughter. She had never approved of Hartleigh's marriage to James Stuart and had always considered Lee Randolph the better catch.

Lee crossed his hands behind his back and faced the women, only to find Elizabeth quizzing the girls about the disposition of his luggage.

The teenagers looked at each other. They'd forgotten the luggage. As often happens around a handsome man, and in the company of a sisterly competitor, good sense had taken a holiday.

It was the young man to their rescue. "I've asked your butler to bring it in," said Lee. "Would you happen to have a houseboy who might assist him?"

Elizabeth rang the small silver bell again. This time a maid appeared at the parlor door.

"Master Lee's luggage."

"Yes, ma'am. I will see it upstairs." After a slight curtsy, she joined the butler and a houseboy on the front porch.

In the parlor, the girls had their heads together, twittering.

"Girls," said Elizabeth, "it's getting late. Time for bed."

The twittering stopped, and furtive glances were exchanged.

"Mrs. Randolph, could Tessa spend the night?"

"Perhaps another time. We do want to make Cousin Lee feel welcome."

"Oh, Cousin Elizabeth," said Lee, winking at the girls, "don't you worry about me."

Oh, but I will. The fox is officially in the henhouse now.

Christian Andersen walked into the parlor, extended a hand, and introduced himself.

"Ah, yes," said Lee. "The Yankee."

"Second Wisconsin Volunteers," said Christian with an easy smile. Christian was sick and tired of being singled out as one of the few Yankees living in Charleston, so he'd fought back on the only terrain Southerners seemed to respect: The War.

"My grandfather was a member of the Iron Brigade." Most Southerners had heard of how the Iron Brigade had fought "Stonewall" Jackson to a standstill at the Second Battle of Bull Run, or Second Manassas, as it was referred to in the South.

More smiling as Christian continued to grip the hand of the Virginian. "Don't tell me. You were named for Robert E. Lee."

"A . . . a distant cousin," stammered the young Virginian.

"Well," said Christian, still holding his hand, "you must be very proud of that branch of the family."

Elizabeth cleared her throat.

Christian dropped the boy's hand, looked at her, but said to Lee. "See you at breakfast."

"You . . . you live here?"

"Just like all the other white folks."

"Christian, would you mind escorting Tessa home?"

"Certainly." Christian thought the south of Broad customs a real hoot. It was like stepping back in time when knights and ladies-in-waiting occupied the world of the Round Table. He headed for the front door.

The phone rang in the hallway again as Tessa left the parlor. Since Christian had preceded her through the double doors of the foyer—Christian hated for servants to open doors for him—the butler was available to answer the phone.

Seconds later, the butler reentered the parlor and said to Elizabeth, "It's for Miss Dory."

Dory moved toward the parlor door. "I'll take it."

"You'll do no such thing!" Elizabeth nodded at Lee Randolph, who stood with his back to the fireplace. "You already have a guest." To the butler: "Please handle this matter."

"No!" moaned the girl, hand rising.

13

"Dory, you forget yourself!"

The girl swallowed hard. Clearing her throat, she said, "I'm sorry." Then to Hartleigh and Lee Randolph, "Please forgive me for being rude."

Elizabeth smiled. "Get your beauty sleep, my dear. If you care to read, fine, but no radio."

"Yes . . . yes, ma'am." After a modified curtsy to Lee Randolph, she said, "By your leave, sir."

Lee nodded, and Dory broke for the hall. As she hurried upstairs, she heard the butler say into the telephone, "I'll be certain to give Miss Campbell your message."

Dory muffled a sob and pulled herself up the stairs by the railing. The butler would do no such thing. He was under strict orders never to offer encouragement to any boy. If young men were interested, they'd stop by and leave a card. It was the only proper way to court a lady, and Elizabeth was determined to make a lady out of Dory Campbell even if it killed the girl.

Topping the stairs, Dory's shoulders slumped as if the weight of the world was on them. Her good fortune of being taken in by this house had turned into the misfortune of being locked up in this tower and with nary a prince in sight.

But with Lee Randolph passing through Charleston on his way to other adventures, perhaps . . . .

THREE

Once outside on the porch, Tessa told Christian that she didn't need to be escorted home.

"You heard Mrs. Randolph." Christian went down the steps ahead of her. At the street, the wrought-iron gate was opened by Gabriel, a young footman. "When one of your elders speaks, it's best to go along to get along."

Tessa followed him out onto the sidewalk, tears welling up in her eyes. She sniffled.

"What's wrong?"

"Nothing. Nothing at all."

Still, Tessa was sobbing by the time they reached the Stuarts' front gate, and Christian had to step lively to open it for her. The Stuarts did not employ a footman, nor did the yardman oil the wrought-iron gate.

"Sure you're okay?" Christian realized he'd not

seen much of Tessa lately. Well, not since his brother had returned up north.

Inside the Stuart's gate, Tessa turned on him. "You do know that you ruined my life."

"Ruined your life?" Christian laughed. "I hardly think so." Teenagers could be so melodramatic.

Tessa raced toward the porch and hustled up the steps with Christian in hot pursuit. Christian knew he couldn't allow their conversation to end on this note, not when the lifeblood of Charleston was gossip.

He took her arm. "Now, see here . . . ."

Sue Ellen rose from the shadows. The girl's aunt had been sitting in the swing with Billy Ray Craven, the assistant county solicitor. Actually, the couple had been kissing in the darkness when the front gate squeaked open. An item of maintenance Sue Ellen forbade the yardman to correct.

Billy Ray leaped from the swing and challenged this man who was chasing Tessa. "You stop right there . . . Christian?"

By now, Tessa was in her aunt's arms and sobbing.

"What's going on?" demanded Sue Ellen in a tone of a woman looking to upbraid a man.

"I was walking her home."

"And part of that exercise was to make her cry?" James Stuart's sister had the same lanky frame, with a small chest and derriere. For this reason she'd been one of the last flappers to embrace the new fashions prescribed by austerity.

"It was something said next door."

"By you?" asked Billy Ray.

"Oh, knock it off." Christian had little patience for fools and Billy Ray had his bona fides in that department. "Mrs. Randolph wanted Tessa escorted home and here I am."

At the mention of this name, Tessa sobbed even louder.

Sue Ellen held Tessa out where she could see her. "What's wrong, girl?"

Tessa shook her head. "I just want to go to my room."

Sue Ellen turned her niece toward the door but said to Christian, "Remain here until I've straightened this out."

"Sorry, but I've got a full day tomorrow."

Billy Ray gave Christian a pleading look.

Christian saw this. "Oh, all right!"

The Yankee fumed as he went over to the swing, sat down, and pulled out a cigar. In a moment, Billy Ray joined him.

They were smoking cigars and talking about the Cardinals' chances of winning another pennant when Sue Ellen returned.

"Be nice to have a major league team in the South," mused Billy Ray.

"Never happen," said Christian, letting out a smoke-filled breath. "Great weather, but you don't have the population base."

Billy Ray laughed. "I can still dream."

"So, where would it be located?"

Both men rose to their feet. "If it's based on population, then it'd have to be Atlanta."

"And the name of the team would be?"

"Easy." Billy Ray laughed. "The Grits."

"Billy Ray," cut in Sue Ellen, "could you give us a minute?"

"Uh-oh." Billy Ray rolled his eyes as he headed for the steps.

"A walk in the park, my boy. You forget I'm married to Rachel Belle." Still, Christian braced himself as he joined Sue Ellen in the porch swing.

"Tessa believes you encouraged your brother to attend the University of Chicago."

"That I did." Christian held his cigar as far away as possible. Women didn't like their odor, and that made cigars even more appealing.

"She believes you sent Luke north to break them up."

Now that got his attention. "Are you serious?"

"When women talk relationships, they're always serious."

"I didn't know that." Christian took a drag off his cigar and blew smoke in Sue Ellen's face. "There was no ring."

Sue Ellen coughed and waved away the smoke. "People don't need a ring to be serious about each other."

Christian glanced at Billy Ray, who stood on the sidewalk, gazing toward the Ashley. "You're telling me."

"Watch your tone, Christian. My husband may be building a dam in Nevada, but my brother still lives here in Charleston."

Flipping the cigar over the banister, Christian got to his feet. "And I have to work with him." Off-handedly he said, "By your leave, madam."

Christian crossed the porch and went down the steps. When he reached the sidewalk, he looked up at her. "And you can tell Tessa that she and Luke being serious never once crossed my mind; otherwise, as a representative of my family, I would've told him to break it off."

"And what does that mean?"

"That Stuart women are much too reckless for my taste."

Back in his bedroom with the baby sleeping and Rachel reading a new mystery, Christian slammed one too many dresser drawers, and the baby cried out.

Without looking up from her story, Rachel said, "You wake him, you rock him."

Christian glanced at the cradle, then sat on his side of the bed. But for that one outburst, the baby remained silent. Still, Christian sat there, shoulders slumped. On the radio Harry Richman sang "I Can't Give You Anything But Love."

Rachel put down her novel. "Very well. What is it?"

"Tessa believes I ruined her life by sending Luke to the University of Chicago."

"That's just plain silly, but teenage girls often think everything's about them." Again, she opened her book.

"She was bawling when I walked her home."

Rachel returned to her new novel, *Mystery Mile,* written by Margery Allingham and featuring the mysterious sleuth Albert Campion. "I'll have a talk with her tomorrow."

"And what will you say?" asked her husband, shifting around on the edge of the bed.

Still looking at the book—Allingham was marvelous at creating eccentric characters—Rachel said, "That you refuse to allow another member of the Andersen family to suffer at the hands of my fellow Charlestonians."

Christian could only stare at her.

His wife turned a page. "And that occasionally you have regrets about your own marriage."

"Now you're the one being silly. I have no such regrets." He kicked off his shoes and lay down beside her.

"Really?" His wife put down her book. "I find that hard to believe."

Christian's hands went under the covers and he

goosed her. Rachel let out a yelp and tried to get away.

"Hey," said her husband, glancing at the bassinette, "you wake him, you rock him."

Elizabeth and Lee Randolph went upstairs while Hartleigh stopped by the study to collect her goodnight kiss, and Hartleigh kissed her husband with enough passion to make him remember her long after she'd left the room.

She was smiling as she climbed the stairs. Marriage was making her into such a wicked person, but what she and James did in the bedroom seemed to please her husband. Hartleigh had the figure of a Gibson girl with a long, elegant neck, a full chest, a wasp waist, and large brown eyes.

She heard the phone ring in the study and cursed under her breath, then chastised herself and followed that by making the sign of the cross. Nothing more to do than go to their room and pick up where she'd left off in Edna Ferber's *Cimarron*.

Before James had proposed marriage, Hartleigh and her mother had lived in what Sue Ellen Stuart called Charleston's Lonely Heart Hotel.

"Get it?" she had said with a grin. "You're the lonely heart." And Sue Ellen repeatedly schemed to slip her best friend out of "this dreary place." It wasn't easy. After Elizabeth had lost her husband, her son, and Hartleigh's twin sister in a ferry boat accident, she had held on tight to the last member of her family.

All that changed when hundreds of men began to pour into Charleston to build the first bridge over the Cooper River and the girls learned that the site engineer would be Sue Ellen's brother. Immediately Sue Ellen began to scheme to get the two of them together: a lonely wallflower and a brother who didn't have his priorities straight.

Upstairs, Lee Randolph was being oriented to the bathroom and whose bedroom was whose.

He smiled as Hartleigh came up the stairs. "I especially wanted to know where you sleep," he said. "I wouldn't want to mistake the bathroom for where a bootlegger sleeps."

Downstairs in the study James picked up the phone. "Yes?"

"James, this is your brother-in-law calling from Las Vegas, Nevada. Can you hear me over this line?"

James leaned forward, hovering over the phone. "Edmund, so good of you to call, but Sue Ellen lives next door. Do you have that number?"

"Yes, I do, but I called you."

James didn't like the sound of that.

"I'm throwing in the towel," said Edmund, his voice rising, "I'm going to divorce your sister."

"What are you talking about? Divorce is illegal in South Carolina."

"But not in Vegas. With the new law out here, it only takes six weeks."

"This is not good, Edmund. It'll cast a shadow over my sister and our family."

"James, your sister's not suited for the life of a camp follower, and the wives of engineers go where their husbands find work." The words tumbled out of Edmund's mouth as if he didn't want to give his brother-in-law an opportunity to cut him off. "There are thousands of unemployed fellows out here in Nevada. We're all living in shacks waiting for Boulder City to be built. Heck, I'd help them build it if that would get me out of Ragtown."

"Ragtown?"

"It's just another Hooverville, but you'd love it. Four divisionary tunnels have to be cut through the mountains to divert the Colorado River before we can start on the concrete gravity-arch."

"Edmund, you're saying that Sue Ellen cannot live under those circumstances . . . what about Las Vegas?"

"Oh, yeah," said Edmund with a laugh, "I want my wife living in Vegas."

"Edmund, these are hard times. Sue Ellen will certainly understand."

"She understood when we were building the bridge over the Cooper River because it was built in her hometown, and she understood when I was working on the Empire State Building and she had a chance to join the Algonquin Roundtable, but this is out in the middle of nowhere. This is the sticks' sticks."

Edmund paused, and James didn't jump in because he had no idea what to say. James was well aware that his sister was a trollop.

"This won't hurt your family's reputation. The House of Stuart is based on a legend that the original James Stuart killed Blackbeard. How can a mere divorce compete with that? In a few years no one will even remember my name."

"I'll remember."

A long pause on the other end of the line, then, "I guess I know what that means. Well, you know where to find me. If I'm lucky I'll be out here seven or eight years." A click, then silence.

"Edmund? Edmund, are you still there?"

No answer.

"Edmund?"

"Captain Stuart, would you like me to try to re-connect?"

James said nothing.

"Captain Stuart?"

"No, Mabel, that won't be necessary."

"I'm sorry, Captain Stuart."

"It's not your fault. It's long distance."

"No, sir. I meant about the divorce."

James gritted his teeth. "Please keep this to yourself. It's going to kill my mother."

"Then don't tell her."

"What? What do you mean?"

"Your sister is in Charleston; her husband's out West—for several years. No one in Charleston has to know."

Once James got off the phone, he called Prescott Mitchell at the Stuart and Company warehouse. James shook his head at this mental error. Rather, the Stuart and Andersen warehouse.

Confined to a wheelchair after a fall off the Cooper River Bridge, Prescott picked up on the first ring. "Warehouse!"

"It's Stuart. Where do you have runs tonight?"

"You ought to spend more time down here, then you'd know."

James let out a long sigh. He could swear that Prescott was his old cocky self, even though confined to a wheelchair.

"When are you leaving?"

"I've got Rock Hill, Spartanburg, and Florence."

"No, Prescott, when are you and Polly returning to Missouri?"

"Us leave? Who said anything about us leaving?"

On his end of the line, James went silent.

"All right then. Polly wants to return to Missouri to avoid another summer in Charleston."

"So how long do I have?"

"You know, you could've promoted me to warehouse manager when you let Eugene Roddy go."

"Prescott, you're in a wheelchair."

"And you couldn't widen the aisles or enlarge the doors so I could roll through them easier?"

"You have a ramp at my mother's."

"You have no faith in me, James."

"You and Polly live downstairs at my mother's house. How much more faith could I have?" James wanted to add that Prescott and his wife lived rent free—Hartleigh's idea—but held back. After all, the man was confined to a wheelchair.

Jiminy, he's right. I think of Prescott as a cripple.

"James, we have plenty of money thanks to you, but Polly doesn't want to be known as a bootlegger's wife."

Now the truth came out. It would appear that Edmund was correct. The House of Stuart was too infamous for a mere divorce to tarnish its reputation.

"We'll talk about this later. Alexander and I'll take the Florence run, but don't let your driver and his shotgun leave before we arrive at the warehouse."

* * *

Leaving Lake City on South Carolina highway 52, a sheriff's deputy pulled them over, and while the deputy fixed his Stetson atop his head, hitched up his pants, and moseyed up to the cab, Alexander and James swapped seats so that Alexander sat behind the wheel.

"Okay, boy," said the deputy, flashing his light in the black man's face. "What you got in here?" With his flashlight, the deputy tapped the rear of the truck.

James leaned forward so the officer could see him. "We're taking a load of hooch to Florence."

"You're rumrunners?" The deputy stepped back and his hand went to his sidearm.

Now James leaned across Alexander and held out a bottle of whiskey. "Would you like a couple of bottles?"

"Mister, I don't drink."

"Of course not, but you know someone, an uncle, or perhaps your father-in-law, who complains about bootleg whiskey tearing up his stomach. This stuff is the bee's knees."

The deputy scratched his jaw, then said, "I'll take it."

The deputy received two bottles; James told his drivers to always give the cops two bottles. With both hands full, they couldn't write a ticket or even write down a license plate number.

FOUR

The following morning, Eileen Stuart noticed that her son seemed rather groggy as he joined her for their daily breakfast together. Eileen's period of mourning was behind her and it was time, according to her friends, for her to rejoin the social scene and meet the remaining eligible men of Charleston, at least those who hadn't jumped out windows after the Panic of '29.

"Did the twins keep you up last night?" asked his mother.

Actually, during the return trip to Charleston, James had been considering the future. He'd had a hand in building the first bridge over the Cooper River, but that job was finished, and as a civil engineer he'd been conditioned to look forward to the next project; the true joy of being an engineer, the new project just around the corner. Running bootlegged liquor would only last until the end of Prohibition, and Prohibition was on its last legs. He needed a project, especially if Christian took over Stuart and Company, rather, Stuart and Andersen.

"James, are you all right?"

"What?" He looked at her. "What did you say?" He had no appetite for shrimp and grits after what he'd seen this morning.

"I asked if the twins kept you up last night."

"No, no. They sleep the whole night through."

His mother smiled. "So what are you going to do next?"

"What do you mean?"

"Oh, please, when you were a child you only focused on the work at hand. Well, I just might have something for you. Would you object to Royce Craven calling on me?" Eileen patted down a fold in the cloth napkin lying across her lap. She did not meet her son's eyes.

"What?" His mind was still on the return trip. James and Alexander had seen farmers, black and white, planting their annual crops of cotton, though there was little market for it.

How many South Carolinians would starve to death this year, or worse, suffer the effects of pellagra from a diet consisting of merely corn? First came the diarrhea and dermatitis; later, dementia, then finally death.

"Royce Craven wishes to marry you?" Now James totally focused on his mother.

"Believe me," said his mother with a chuckle, "when men and women of my age court, it's with the intent of matrimony."

"I see. Then that goal should be considered when-ever discussing this issue."

"Yes," said his mother with a laugh. "I believe so."

She'd been anxious about this conversation. The social graces weren't her middle child's strongest suit, but James did have a strong sense of duty. And his wife had been raised by a very demanding Elizabeth Randolph. James would have little problem minding his p's and q's.

"You do know that such a marriage would give Mister Craven the ownership of this house and access to the money produced by the trust fund Daddy set up for you."

"I know my responsibilities as a bride, James. I've done this all before. There must be a dowry."

"Your assets are larger than any usual dowry."

"Yet they are my assets, and by custom they will be controlled by my husband."

James leaned back in his chair. "Then I should meet with Mister Craven."

"Of course, but perhaps you could confide in me as to your concerns."

James stared into his plate. His shrimp and grits were getting cold. "Well, you're . . . you're known around town as—"

"A rich widow?"

"Er . . . yes, ma'am."

"Then it's your duty to lower those expectations."

"And I'm prepared to do so."

"This is why I bring this matter to your attention. Your brother or sister would've bungled this, and I wouldn't want Mister Craven to be frightened off."

James realized his mother was seriously considering marrying Royce Craven, which opened another can of worms. "You do remember that Billy Ray and Sue Ellen were once engaged."

"Goodness gracious, James, that was years ago, and both of them are married."

James did not have the nerve to pursue this line of inquiry. Hopefully, Sue Ellen would change her ways when she understood their mother's happiness was at stake. And perhaps pigs would fly.

"The House of Stuart is guided by Morgan's rules of booty, and all hands receive an equal share; the captain, who's responsible for the good repair of the ship and its next project, receives five or six shares; other officers, two shares, but your former husband is no longer a member of the crew."

"And I'm quite confident you'll make that clear to Mister Craven. There's no windfall here, only a steady flow of income."

"And you're sure Mister Craven harbors no illusions of participating in the family business?"

"That, too, must be made clear to any and all beaus."

James smiled. "You sound as if you're going to keep me busy."

"James, there's no reason to be vulgar."

His face lost its smile. "Yes, ma'am."

"And I don't want piles of cash lying around this house anymore. I've found currency on the tables, stacked on shelves in the closets, and taking up space in dresser drawers. Even the servants have been pressed into service counting money. All I want in this house is my pin money."

Which was why, two days later, James lunched with Royce Craven at a speakeasy overlooking the wharfs. Farther upriver stood the bridge: one hundred and fifty feet tall at its highest point; two lanes of traffic, both lanes ten feet wide and with no barrier between lanes.

Since the opening of the bridge, it had become a rite of passage to attempt to drive over the bridge without your car overheating or losing your nerve. Racing down from the pinnacle, small children screamed as if riding a rollercoaster, and there had been several wrecks when fathers had turned around to chastise their offspring and drifted into the oncoming lane.

Royce Craven had been one of the Charlestonians who'd said the bridge "had certainly ruined a perfectly beautiful harbor." Probably for that reason, Royce seated himself so that James would see the harbor entrance, not the upriver bridge. He was a fit, balding man of fifty-eight, tanned from his daily round of golf.

"Many times I've watched you win the cup from a seat on High Battery. The whole family would be there. We'd set up card tables and cover them with fried chicken, a pig, shrimp and grits, large pots of frogmore stew, and all the trimmings. Everyone was invited: in-laws, outlaws, and friends."

Royce became serious. "I've missed that, James, and I want it again with your mother. She deserves a second chance after all she's gone through. Don't you agree?"

Evidently, Royce wanted to address the elephant in the room: his dead father. But the older man's efforts went for naught as James thought he saw a familiar face across the room.

Dory Campbell.

What was that child doing in a speak?

"James?"

"Sorry," said James, returning his attention to Royce Craven. "Thought I saw someone I knew." He shook out his napkin. Rather perfunctorily, he asked, "Did you ever race?"

"Never. Horses were my family's passion. Actually, my father was one of the few remaining members when the club voted to dissolve itself and dispose of its assets." The older man let out a long sigh. "A bitter pill to swallow when Aiken was opening their new training facility."

A waiter took their drink order.

"Beer," said James, looking over Royce's shoulder. Was that really Dory Campbell? She was supposed to be in school.

"Beer," agreed Royce.

Returning his attention to his potential stepfather, he said, "My mother says you're an excellent bridge player."

Royce shrugged. "People my age try to keep their wits about them. You know the sad tale of the Ingram family. I was playing at an adjoining table when Lois had trouble with her bidding. Since I was the dummy, I leaned over to give her some help. Lois was never the same after that game, and I'm not sure if that wasn't what caused William's heart attack. That or the market crash."

He took the beer offered to him by the waiter. "I lost everything. Not like you. You got out in time."

James shrugged. "Just lucky."

"Oh, yes," said Royce, chuckling, "and I'd like to hear how that luck happened. People at my club speculate about it all the time. You became a very rich young man."

Again James shrugged.

"Oh, come on, James. What's the harm? It's not like the market will ever recover in my lifetime."

"You don't think the market will come back?" When anyone discussed the economy, James always had time to listen. He subscribed to both the *Wall Street Journal* and the *Financial Times*, though same-day delivery was impossible.

"It's been almost two years," said Royce, "and you can't find anyone who's returned to the stock market. Well, if he has, the fool wouldn't mention it. Best to move on to greener pastures."

"And that would be?"

Royce chuckled. "Oh, that's not for an old man

like me to say. My generation was finished by this crash." He shook out his napkin. "The world belongs to you young people. You'll decide where the next fortunes will be made."

"Fortunes made after such a panic? Now where would that particular opportunity be?"

Royce sipped his beer. "I have every confidence in you, my boy."

James looked beyond the older man and saw the girl who looked like Dory Campbell laugh. Who was she with?

"Your mother can't stop bragging about you," went on Royce, "and I'm of an age where you only want to know that your children have married, have decent jobs, and aren't in prison."

"Ready to order, gentlemen?" asked the waiter.

Looking up from spreading the linen napkin across his lap, Royce said, "I'm paying for this."

"Nonsense. I invited you."

"Then you go first." A universal ploy where the one paying for the meal reveals to his guest how much money the guest is allowed to spend for his own meal.

James ordered she-crab soup, the lima bean dinner, and another beer when the current one ran out. Royce quickly followed, ordering fried chicken along with okra soup. Both men requested bread pudding for dessert. The waiter didn't ask for the return of menus because there were none. When you came into this particular speakeasy, you knew exactly what you wanted, and if you were a newcomer, you could try to decipher a menu scribbled on a blackboard near the front door.

The speak was jammed from pillar to post and a low hum ran throughout the room. A bar served liquor but most patrons came for the food, the selection pure Charleston, and most often, from the sea.

Determined to elicit a response from James, Royce put down his beer. "You know, your father was one crazy son of a bitch."

"And my sister inherited all that recklessness."

Royce regarded James but graciously said, "I heard Sue Ellen had returned to Charleston."

"Which means I have some babysitting to do. You too."

"Me?"

"Your son and my sister will be in dangerously close proximity if you should marry my mother."

Once his soup was served, James said, "Anything you've heard about flappers rings true when it comes to my little sister." James looked the older man in the eye. "And I mean anything."

Royce sipped from his okra soup. He'd read *The Great Gatsby* and would believe anything regarding flappers. "And if I should object to something your sister wishes to do?"

"You can't anymore whip Sue Ellen into shape than you can stop your son from coming around."

The older man put down his spoon. "What are you insinuating?"

"I'm not insinuating. Your son and my sister were once engaged, and the torch never went out."

"But Billy Ray's married."

"And the fool thinks he can run for public office. But his dalliance with my sister will sink any political future. Nowadays everyone owns a Brownie camera and can Kodak the moment of their compromising situation."

"And Grace?"

"There's a reason why your daughter-in-law is called the Sherry Queen of Charleston."

"But Grace wants to live in the governor's mansion. She used to visit her grandfather there."

"I don't think that's possible." James leaned

forward and lowered his voice. "Any combining of our families will at some point include a proud and angry young man when your son is found out by the people of Charleston. That's when things can really go off the rails."

"Does your mother know any of this?"

"If she did, what could she possibly do?"

"You make it sound so hopeless."

"All Stuarts are hopeless reprobates." James dipped his spoon into his she-crab soup. Could that really be Dory Campbell sitting over there? He wouldn't know for sure unless he confronted her.

"You don't fit the Stuart mold, do you?"

"What?" James looked at Royce. "Oh, I'm too much like my mother. That's why I was able to get out of the market in time. I spook easily."

"That still doesn't explain your timing. How did you get spooked at just the right time?"

James sighed. This whole conversation about the market was becoming rather tiresome. Still, perhaps he could use Royce Craven to spread the word that it had all been dumb luck.

"One day the fellow at the gas station was filling up my car, rather, while he was washing my windshield, he recommended a stock, then the bagger at Piggy Wiggly recommended another, and before I arrived home, a newsie at the traffic light touted a different stock. I got out of the market the very next day."

Royce stared at him.

"True story." On the other side of the room, the girl who looked like Dory Campbell was having a cigarette lit by . . . was that Hartleigh's cousin Lee Randolph leaning over to light the girl's smoke? If so, the boy certainly moved fast.

Royce began laughing, then coughing, and he coughed long enough for the waiter to offer him a glass of water.

Royce waved him off. "Oh, that's rich." Tears ran down his cheeks and he wiped them away. "No one at my club suspected anything as simple as keeping your ear to the ground." He coughed again. "Everyone thought you had inside information." Royce cleared his throat and sipped from his beer again.

James shrugged. What people thought of him was not half as important as the women he felt responsible for. James put down his napkin as their soup bowls were replaced by their entrees.

"Royce," said James, getting to his feet, "please continue with your meal. I need to check on something."

"In the middle of your meal?"

"I'm afraid so."

"Is there a problem?" asked the waiter.

"I want to speak to the owner."

The waiter appeared puzzled.

"Now!"

The waiter led James over to the bar where a large man laughed with his customers.

The large man on the other side of the bar straightened up. "Yes, Captain Stuart." He gave his waiter the evil eye. "What can I do for you?"

"I think you have a schoolgirl in here. Could you call the truant officer?"

"Absolutely." The owner lifted the phone and spoke into it. "Mabel, I have a schoolgirl loitering around my place. Please send over the truant officer." The owner nodded, then hung up. "Five minutes. One works Market Street." He looked over the room of crowded tables. "Where's the girl?"

"No need to make a scene. Let me pull her out of here."

The owner gestured at his bouncer at the other end of the bar. "Well, give us the high sign if you need any help."

James crossed the floor to the table where Dory Campbell and her fellow sat. Sitting across from her, and with his back to James, was the Virginia cousin of Elizabeth Randolph. Randolph had broad shoulders, a thin mustache, and wore a loose single-breasted suit. An unruly mop of curly brown hair covered his head. He was a small man, about five and a half feet tall.

Without preamble, James asked, "Why are you not in school?"

The two young people looked up at him.

"It's none of your concern, James," said Dory Campbell, returning her attention to Lee Randolph.

"You're not old enough to call me by my first name."

The young man stood, smiled, and stuck out his hand. "You must be the bootlegger. I'm Lee Randolph."

James did not take the boy's hand. "Ah, yes, the young man who sleeps under my roof but has yet to introduce himself."

Lee continued to smile. "Well, we do have different hours." When he saw the look on James's face, he became more serious. "I'm sorry, sir, but I've been busy with relatives. There are a good number of Randolphs in Charleston, as you know."

"And, it would appear, encouraging schoolgirls to play hooky. During the time it took you to locate this speak, you could've dropped by my office."

"Sorry, sir, but I don't want people to think *I'm* a bootlegger."

James's eyes narrowed. "Who recommended this speak?"

"The solicitor, Billy Ray Craven."

There was that name again. This foolishness had to be stamped out immediately. Even Royce Craven would agree to that.

"Well, Lee, you truly are a fool."

"Pardon me?" The smile vanished from his face.

"Dory Campbell is not yet sixteen years old, and not only that, my wife's mother, your cousin, pulled a lot of strings to get this ungrateful child into Ashley Hall."

Dory glared up at him. "You can't speak about me in that tone of voice."

James glanced over his shoulder and saw a man in a black suit weaving his way through the crowded tables.

When he arrived, the truant officer asked, "Is this the young lady to be returned to Ashley Hall?" The truant officer had to be careful, as his supervisor always reminded him that there were no truants living south of Broad.

Dory threw down her napkin. "This is ridiculous! I'm not this man's property."

"That's correct. You belong with your family in Summerville, and that's where you'll be returned if you don't leave with this officer immediately."

"You can't do this!" shouted Dory, drawing the attention of those seated around her. "Please don't do this!"

But James was already returning to his table.

People stared as Dory was led away by the truant officer, and Lee caught up with James as he wove his way through the tables.

Lee seized James's shoulder and turned him around. "You, sir, are a cad. You didn't have to embarrass the young lady in front of all these people."

James stared at the hand, and very quickly Lee's hand slid from James's shoulder.

"And you, sir, are practically homeless. But fear not, there's a Hooverville in North Charleston waiting for young men just like you who don't officially present themselves."

The speakeasy's owner and his bouncer were there, both easily twice the size of Randolph. The bouncer took Lee's arm and escorted him toward the door.

Looking back, Lee shouted, "Believe me, Stuart, you've not heard the last of this!"

Of course not, and I'm sure you'll go running to my mother-in-law with some song and dance.

The owner of the speakeasy said, "Neither you nor Mister Craven will be charged for this meal. I appreciate what you did."

"Thank you." James returned to his table and sat down.

"What was that all about?" asked Royce.

Again, James shook out his napkin. Their meals had been removed and were now being returned from the kitchen.

"Dirty laundry, but you'll learn all about it while courting my mother." James remembered what he had meant to ask Craven. "Royce, how well do you know Solicitor Leon Harris?"

FIVE

After lunch, the two men returned to negotiating the dowry.

"I know the Stuarts aren't that much interested in land, but that's what the Cravens bring to this union and plenty of it." Royce pushed away his plate with the remains of the fried chicken, then leaned forward and lowered his voice. "The Craven family is one of the most land-poor families in the low country. When I lost everything in the market, I lost my cash flow and I don't have the money to cover the taxes, that is, without a sympathetic banker such as your father."

"And my father's no longer there."

"Actually, there aren't many sympathetic bankers around these days. I'm sorry. I didn't mean that to sound so cold-blooded."

James shook his head. "No offense taken."

Royce studied the younger man. "Are you aware that Craven County was one of the three original counties established by the Lords' Proprietors?"

"I'm not much up on landlubber history." For over two hundred years, the Stuart family had found their opportunities at sea. For instance, all James knew about agriculture was that the boll weevil had recently passed through, and much like Sherman, with devastating results.

"Craven County no longer exists, but when it did, Craven County *was* South Carolina. Colleton and Berkeley counties were Johnnies-come-lately; then the state did away with counties in favor of districts, then swung back to counties again. Somewhere along the way, Craven County was lost forever."

Royce pulled several sheets of paper from his inside coat pocket and laid them beside James's plate: deeds for land in Dorchester, Berkeley, and Charleston counties; the holdings were vast, inland plantations James would never have associated with the Craven family.

From the other inside coat pocket, Royce produced tax notices. "I've already lost the farm in Dorchester County; soon the land in Berkeley and Charleston counties will go on the block. I need cash to pay off these taxes or the tracts will be sold at auction. Your father did what he could, but his bank went under, and with the reorganization of its assets, the tax collector is hot on my trail."

"It's the mayor pro tem, Burnet Maybank. Lewis Belle says politicians always elect an Episcopalian when they want to get something done, and Burnet Maybank's scouring every nook and cranny to keep Charleston from going bankrupt." James studied the notices, then looked up. "Do you have an estimate of your obligations?"

From under his eyebrows, Royce looked at James. "At least eight thousand dollars."

James whistled. "That's quite a bit of money."

"And if I don't have it by the first of the year, the control of my family's remaining property will pass into the hands of accountants in some bank, probably up north."

"What are you proposing, Royce?"

"If I had access to the Stuart money, which I suspect is not always being put to work, we could hold onto that property."

At this point in the negotiations, James took a moment to explain Morgan's rules of booty, which meant that Royce Craven would never own any shares unless he went to work for Stuart and Company.

"My mother receives nothing from Stuart and Company. Her money comes from a trust fund left behind by my father. Now, Royce, are you capable of pitching in?"

"James, let's be honest. If I could manage my own affairs in this economy, do you think I'd be here negotiating your mother's dowry?"

That stopped James, and it became his turn to ponder the situation. Without another word, James produced a checkbook from his breast pocket and wrote a check for eight thousand dollars. He handed it to Royce.

"What's this?" asked Royce as the bread pudding arrived.

"With your taxes paid, you'll have more time to think about my mother's future, not your past."

"James," said Royce, folding the check and sticking it inside his wallet, "I'm going to pay back every penny of this."

"Don't worry about it. Just take good care of my mother."

"Coffee, gentlemen?" asked the waiter.

"Black."

"Black."

Once their waiter left, another waiter pulled a pistol from his waistband and waved it overhead as he turned round and round in the middle of the tables.

"The rich must pay! They must be *made* to pay! There's no fairness in this world if the rich don't pay! Down with the rich!"

James slipped from his chair, stepped over behind the waiter during one of his turns, and buffaloed the man across the back of his head with one of his Webleys.

The waiter's arm came down, he dropped his weapon, and his legs wobbled. By this time, James had holstered his pistol and grabbed the waiter under the arms, lowering him to the floor. Another customer kicked away the pistol; plenty of males were on their feet, guns drawn. Seconds later, the bouncer had the waiter's hands tied behind him and the owner announced to the room that dessert was on the house.

After holstering their weapons, several patrons saluted James for his quick thinking; a few, of course, groused that they could've taken the waiter with a single shot from across the room. Their loved ones trembled and suggested that it would be much safer to have their luncheon at home.

Hearing this from an adjoining table, Royce muttered, "That's not going to help the economy recover." After showing his pistol to James, Royce put away the weapon. "Bought it a few weeks ago."

"Royce, I do believe we're finished here." He tossed a dollar on the table, and they left the speakeasy.

Stepping out on Market Street, James asked, "Ever fire that new weapon of yours?"

"I'm a shotgun man, really, quail hunter."

"Do me a favor then. Leave that pistol at home until I have a chance to teach you how to handle it properly. It's not just suicides that are on the rise, it's family members shooting each other when someone comes home late or arrives without notice."

James jerked a thumb over his shoulder. "There were enough weapons in that speakeasy to seize a banana republic. I'm surprised I wasn't shot, along with the anarchist."

While James was making arrangements for his mother to be courted, Lee Randolph returned lickety-split to his cousin's home to confess his transgression. There he found Elizabeth, Hartleigh, and Rachel about to leave for an afternoon of bridge and sherry at Georgiana Belle's, the heralded Belle family townhouse.

These days, Hartleigh remained in a perpetual state of exhaustion. Never had she participated in so many engagements, well, not since the last time Rachel had resided under this roof. Hartleigh didn't know how Rachel kept up this level of activity— she belonged to every club known to women—and occasionally wondered why she chose to lead such a hectic life.

"Ah, there you are, my dear cousins, and Mrs. Andersen." Lee half bowed, which the two younger women returned with modified curtsies.

Slightly flushed, Lee rushed through his explanation. "I've just been thrown out of a speak because I was there with an underage girl who said she had no school today."

Pausing only to catch his breath, Lee continued. "And who do you think this vixen was? It was our own Dory Campbell. She found me wandering up and down King Street. Women's clothing has changed radically in the last year, not so much, the men's.

So, dear cousin, I'm prepared to pay any penance you demand, but honestly, doesn't Dory appear to be eighteen?"

Such a tour de force by such a skillful practitioner put the three women back on their heels.

All Elizabeth could ask was, "Dory played hooky today?"

Hartleigh said nothing. She was completely taken in, and Rachel's stomach was in knots from anticipating her first face-to-face meeting with her new sister-in-law in over a month. Up the street, on High Battery, workmen crawled all over her sister-in-law's former home; you'd have to be blind not to notice it.

"Well," said Elizabeth, "we're certainly not going to flog you for such a transgression."

"No, no," said Hartleigh, smiling. "You've done nothing more than any other young man would do in such circumstances. Isn't that so, Mother?"

But her mother was thinking: if those *were* the actual circumstances.

"Looking back, perhaps I should've been more suspicious because Dory was shopping without a companion, but this was King Street. There were all sorts of women, young and old, shopping among the establishments that have yet to close."

"So," asked Elizabeth, "Dory finally admitted her age?"

A pained look crossed Lee's face. "Not exactly. A truant officer stopped by our table and worried the truth out of her."

The butler appeared at the parlor door. "Alexander is here with the automobile, ma'am."

"Thank you." To Lee, she said, "I will speak to Dory when she returns from school. She did return to school, didn't she?"

"Absolutely! There's no doubt of that. Once her

true age was revealed, I insisted that she be returned to Ashley Hall."

"Very well."

The three women left the house, and once the Buick disappeared down the street, Lee had the butler call a taxi, then he raced off to the Stuart and Company warehouse.

So, when James returned from lunch, his office manager, Prescott Mitchell, told him that the new guy from Richmond was out back loading cartons of liquor into trucks.

"A new guy from Richmond? Whatever do you mean?"

"Lee Randolph."

"Oh." James looked through the glass and tried to see the dock from where he stood. Impossible with all the cartons stacked ceiling high.

"He said he'd never ever worked for a bootlegger before."

"I suppose not." James had nothing against a kid learning from his mistakes and making amends. "Did someone check him out?"

"I thought you had," said the man in the wheelchair. "You're the one who recommended him."

"Uh-huh. Get Christian in here, would you?"

Prescott used the new Marconi public address system to call the warehouse manager into the office. James had overhauled his father's distribution system, installing a diesel-powered forklift and an IBM tabulating machine to track inventory. In a building in North Charleston, a trucking company kept a fleet of Mack trucks in good repair, and in the state capital, two attorneys busily lobbied for better roads.

Once Christian arrived, James asked, "What do you think of the new man?"

"Won't last the day." Christian wiped his forehead with a handkerchief. "He's too small and never done any manual labor. I know you try to hire as many able-bodied men as possible, but he's more likely to get injured than contribute." Christian took a seat on the corner of the wooden table. "Why'd you think he'd work out?"

"It's not a job but an apology. Randolph believes he insulted me and he's trying to smooth things over."

"But you don't care what people think."

"I do care if they're revenuers."

"Revenuers?" Christian came off the table.

"I want Randolph checked out. Both of you were taken in, and I want to make sure we're doing everything possible to protect the livelihood of the families dependent on us."

Reaching for a steno pad, Prescott said, "Then give me the particulars and I'll contact the Pinkertons."

"While you're at it, even if it requires employing another agent, include surveillance of Billy Ray Craven."

SIX

Over the next few days, the Pinkerton agent followed Lee Randolph from one brothel to another, watched as he gambled away a small fortune, or drank himself under the table at a variety of speakeasies. The young man picked up girls easier than a blue serge suit picked up lint, seemed to have an incredible run of bad luck at the gaming tables, but always had money waiting for him at the Western Union, though Lee pled a shortage of funds whenever he traveled in the company of others.

Lee appeared to be close to assistant solicitor Billy Ray Craven, who would drink and gamble with young Randolph but never accompany him to a bordello. The Pinkerton had to admire Billy Ray for his fidelity to his wife, an attractive young woman who dressed in the latest fashions and knocked back liquor as well as any man. The reddish-brown-haired woman had long legs, small breasts, and the Pinkerton overheard her called "Sue Ellen."

His reports were given orally to a bootlegger by the name of James Stuart, who never appeared surprised until he heard the name of Billy Ray's wife. Then there had been a hardening of the eyes and a setting of the jaw. Evidently, the bootlegger must've learned what he wanted to know because the following day surveillance was discontinued and new instructions issued.

As one of the Pinkertons boarded a train for out west, Royce Craven hosted a luncheon for twenty men interested in exploring a run by Solicitor Leon W. Harris in the Democratic primary. The luncheon was held in a conference room at the Charleston Hotel, and though the luncheon drew only twenty people, as Royce pointed out, they were seasoned pols of the bourbon persuasion who would have to be convinced that a progressive candidate could win nomination to the United States Senate.

Billy Ray gave the welcoming address, and James could only sit there and marvel at how such a fiery speaker could be turned into a lap dog by his sister. The two men didn't speak, except when Royce pulled them together for a photograph. Under those circumstances, James and Billy Ray shook hands, and Royce, grinning, stood behind them, a hand on each young man's shoulder.

The winner of the Democratic primary, or its resultant runoff, would be the next senator from South Carolina. Republicans rarely ran in opposition, not since Governor Wade Hampton had made it perfectly clear to President Ulysses Grant that former officers of the Confederacy now ran South Carolina and that the state would be casting its six electoral votes for the Democratic candidate, Samuel J. Tilden.

So electoral votes were exchanged for the removal of the last federal troops from South Carolina and Rutherford B. Hayes followed Grant into the White House. Wade Hampton and his aging Confederates also guaranteed that the freedmen would always have access to the polls.

The former Confederates kept their word. Unfortunately, "Pitchfork" Ben Tillman and his generation were not a party to this agreement, nor were any of their political descendants. So the long years of Jim Crow settled in over Carolina and the winner of the Democratic primary became the next senator from South Carolina.

Once the meals had been finished and the small talk done—most of the chatter centering on whether the Citadel would ever beat Clemson College again— Lewis Belle opened the discussion. Anytime you could have a Belle of Charleston on the dais, you were way ahead of the game.

"Coley Blease always carries the Holy City because of his laissez-faire attitude toward how we run things down here." Lewis meant that the brothels, gambling dens, and bootleggers were given a pass. "But Charleston needs more than benign neglect."

"Agreed," said William Rhett, a descendant of the firebrand who had led South Carolina out of the Union in 1861. "This state needs someone to go to Washington, turn on the money faucet, and run a hose down here to South Carolina."

Several men chuckled, but James Stuart only stared at Rhett. This was what Jim Byrnes had meant about the cotton farmers and textile workers having their backs to the wall. South Carolina was broke and a long, dark future lay before it. Was that the kind of world he wished to leave to the twins?

Rhett continued. "Governor Manning improved the farm market, paved the roads, and set the government on tax cheaters, proving that local government can work for the common good."

Royce glanced at James and said a silent prayer of thanks that his back taxes had been paid.

At the podium Lewis Belle laughed. "Your ancestor's spinning in his grave, Rhett."

"Times have changed, Lewis. Farmers can't sell their crops, the textile mills are shutting down, and people are being thrown out of their homes."

"And all this affects you how?" asked Lewis, playing the devil's advocate. "Your family comes from money."

Rhett raised a finger to make his point. "The homeless of South Carolina are like Coxey's Army marching on Washington in '94 and '14. Sooner or later, they're going to figure out that they don't have to go all the way to Washington to pick a fight. I own property in this state, and unlike my ancestor, I'm not willing to watch it burn. And this time it won't be the Yankees doing the burning but our own kin."

Several men glanced at Christian Andersen.

"No offense, Christian."

The Yankee nodded. "None taken."

"And the people in this state own guns," added Rhett. "They own one hell of a lot of guns."

Christian had to agree. Growing up in Wisconsin there had always been guns around the house, but the number of guns held by Southerners, well, it was like these Rebs expected the Union Army to show up on their doorstep in the middle of the night.

And why not? Hadn't the Union Army done that before.

"We need someone other than Coley Blease in Washington," finished Rhett. "Sure, Coley will leave well enough alone, but is that what's best for our state, especially with all the strikes happening in the cotton mills?" Rhett was referring to the increasing number of textile workers protesting the "stretch out."

To counter lower prices on the world market, the mill owners demanded that their employees increase the number of looms they ran and forgo all breaks. The owners also had begun paying a piece rate despite how long it took to finish a particular job, and instead of using profits to raise wages, they had hired more supervisors to keep an eye on workers.

"Balderdash!" said an elderly guest. "There was no deal with Grant. The military governor of South Carolina informed the president that it would take an army larger than the one the Union had fielded during the war to complete the reconstruction of South Carolina. For this reason, federal troops were removed. It wasn't due to some vote-swapping scheme."

Several men rolled their eyes.

My lord, thought Royce Craven, Charlestonians couldn't get together without an argument breaking out about the war—an advantage missed here, an opportunity missed there, and a general whitewashing of the facts.

"I'm with Rhett," said Lewis Belle. "We need fresh representatives in Congress. We need someone like Leon Harris."

"What about Jimmy Byrnes?" asked someone.

"Aw," said Lewis, "the only thing Jimmy did for this state was to get US 1 run through his wife's hometown of Aiken."

Many laughed. Still, it was nice to have US 1 run through the state so the Yankees and their tin lizzies would pass through on their way to Florida. But Yankees didn't always stop in South Carolina. Many of them avoided it like the plague.

"We need money to rebuild our state and attract tourists." Lewis looked around the room. "We need to seriously consider someone like Leon Harris."

Tessa and Dory were walking to their piano lesson when they got into it again, plowing the same old ground that had separated them from the moment Lee Randolph had arrived in Charleston.

"Remember, I saw Lee first," said Dory. "You stay away from him. He's my boyfriend."

"Lee spoke to me first so that makes him my boyfriend," countered Tessa.

"You already have a boyfriend."

"He's in Chicago."

"Well, I've held hands with Lee," bragged Dory. "It must be serious."

"I have, too."

"In public?"

"Of course not. A lady never displays affection in public."

Smirking, Dory added, "I let him kiss me."

Tessa stopped, gripping her music book across her chest. "You didn't! I don't believe you."

"Believe me." Dory moved off down the sidewalk.

Tessa strode after her. "It's a sin to tell a lie."

"If you get caught, and Lee and I've never been caught."

"It's still a sin. God sees you."

"Oh, don't be such a square or you'll never ever neck with anyone."

"Neck?" Tessa stopped. "Why . . . why would I do that? I'm not engaged."

"Necking feels good," said Dory pridefully, "and boys like it. If you'd necked with Luke, he'd probably still be in Charleston."

"Luke had to go off to college."

"Oh, yes. I'm sure that's why he left."

Dory left Tessa standing there, but ten feet down the sidewalk, Dory faced Tessa again as the former runaway walked backwards down the sidewalk. "Think about it."

Tessa did, and it was only after Dory disappeared into the piano teacher's house that Tessa began to trudge down the street after her.

What Dory had said couldn't be true. Lee Randolph was sweet, and she trusted him. He wouldn't have betrayed her!

And Dory had been caught playing hooky. Dory bragged that she'd been caught in a speakeasy with Lee Randolph. Nobody believed her. How would a girl their age sneak into a speak?

Tessa nodded to herself. Probably the worst Dory had done was to smoke a few cigarettes. No. Dory wasn't being truthful.

Tessa became aware of a car following her. A dark Buick pulled ahead of her and stopped. Uncle James got out, closing the door behind him.

Alarmed, she asked, "Is something wrong?"

"Not at all. Saw you walking down the street and decided to join you. Is that all right?"

"Well, of course." Tessa gestured up the street at the door Dory had disappeared into. "My lesson is in that block so it won't be a very long walk."

They walked along in silence. In truth Tessa hadn't had many conversations with her Uncle James, well, not since the night he had rescued her from rumrunners while she and Luke had been swimming in the buff off the Isle of Palms. It was downright embarrassing to even think about it. Could that be why Luke didn't write more often?

Crossing the street, she asked, "Is this about Mister Andersen?"

James had no idea what in the world the girl was talking about.

"It's nothing," explained Tessa. "Mrs. Andersen had a word of prayer with me about how her husband hadn't intentionally set out to ruin my life."

James gaped at her. What in the devil had he gotten himself into? He glanced at the Buick moving steadily ahead of them. No help there. Alexander merely grinned from the window of the Buick. He appeared to be amused at James's predicament.

"I thought Mister Andersen sent Luke away to break us up."

James nodded with a jerk of his head.

"He didn't even know Luke and I were serious. Oh, we still write, but I have no idea if this is a formal courtship or not, and in truth, who would Luke discuss courting with?" She glanced at him. "What was it you wanted to talk about?"

James had to remember why he was here. "I wanted to pay you a compliment."

Tessa smiled. "How sweet of you."

James didn't know about that but knew for a fact that he was in over his head. What in blue blazes would he do when the twins became teenagers?

Tessa was still smiling and waiting for her compliment.

"Hartleigh says I need to tell you how proud I am of you."

"Well, thank you, Uncle James."

"She thinks . . . she thinks such praise is overdue."

"Oh," said Tessa, chuckling, "compliments can very well be past due, but you don't see me refusing one."

Cripes, thought James. She's trying to make this easy on me. Is that what girls were put on earth to do? Grease the skids?

"I know Stuart women have it much tougher than the men. We men can go around being real horses' asses and never give it another thought, but you're a girl and there'll be people trying to bring you down."

His niece frowned. "Bring me down?"

James's hands were restless. He didn't know what to do with them. Finally, he jammed them into his pants pockets. "Oh, you know, take advantage of you or think you're a woman of loose morals because you're a Stuart." There, he'd said it.

"Uncle James, what in the world are you talking about? People have always been nice to me, despite my circumstances."

"I'm just saying . . . that you need to know about men."

A nervous smile appeared on Tessa's face. "Is this the birds and the bees talk?" Her face reddened.

James's hands came up as if to fend off such an idea. "Oh, no! That would be in Hartleigh's domain. What I'm talking about is scalphunters."

"Scalphunters?"

"Er . . . men who . . . try to . . ." James glanced away. "I don't know how to put this . . ." But James did know how to put it. He simply couldn't bring himself to use such coarse language in front of this virginal teen.

"What I'm trying to say is that as you go through life you'll occasionally meet some Don Juan who hopes you won't hold him to such high standards." Feeling he'd hit his stride, James went on to add, "And I'm proud to say that you've never taken up with someone below your station."

The girl wasn't responding, so James continued. "Someone like Luke Andersen has proven his worth by attending the University of Chicago. You know, that kind of a boy."

And with that, James leaned over, gave his niece a peck on the cheek, and fled to the Buick where he told Alexander to return to the warehouse and be quick about it.

Again Tessa was left standing on the sidewalk wondering what had just happened. She'd have to sort this out, even though she understood that Uncle James approved of Luke.

She must dash off a letter to him. As to Lee Randolph, well, it never hurt to have a boyfriend in waiting. Still, she wished Luke would write more often. They seemed to have so much in common.

SEVEN

A couple of days later, Royce Craven parked his car next to the open doors of the Stuart and Company warehouse, and as he got out, a cop ambled over. Four men were hauling a sign into the warehouse, and two ladders stood outside, flanking the double doors. The sign read:

Stuart and Andersen
Moving and Storage

Summoned by the cop, Alexander soon appeared at the double doors and escorted Royce into the building. The two men wove their way past furniture covered with paper that filled the front of the warehouse and an overhead bin. Behind the furniture sat an office, and then rows and rows of liquor boxes. The walls of the office were glass from the waist up, and Royce saw James and Christian arguing in front of a third man in a wheelchair.

Royce had never considered the actual size and scope of this operation, but it was huge and operating smoothly as orders were filled for customers and shipped throughout the entire state. Royce stopped following Alexander and watched as a mechanical tractor with a vertical lifting mast moved cartons of liquor from a tall stack to the loading dock at the rear of the building.

Uh-huh. He'd made the right decision to throw in with the House of Stuart.

Alexander wandered back to him. "That's a forklift, Mister Royce," explained the black man. "Saves on labor costs and no one strains their back."

Royce nodded and followed the large black man over to the office. Every white man south of Broad knew who Alexander was: the always polite and well-dressed Negro who was treated like one of the boys. And white men did not cross the Stuarts on this issue, for if white folks were to honor the history of Charleston, it also required honoring the fact that pirates were treated equally, as were all shipmates of the House of Stuart.

When Alexander opened the door to the office, they heard James say: " . . . before I went to all that trouble of having the sign made."

James sat behind a large desk, the fellow in the wheelchair manned the wooden table, and across from the table stood a pair of bunk beds. Royce had heard his daughter-in-law speak of the necessity for bunk beds as her family grew, but he'd never actually seen a pair. Some wet-behind-the-ears kid in a black suit, white shirt, and dull tie sat on the lower bunk bed and watched Christian's chewing out. Overhead a fan turned slowly.

The man in the wheelchair rolled out from behind the table. "Yes, sir, what can I do for you?"

"James . . . if he's not busy."

"Royce, good to see you." James stood up, reached across the desk, and shook hands. He glanced at the wet-behind-the-ears young man but said to Royce, "Have you seen our operation?"

"No." The older man glanced through the glass wall. "Can't say that I have."

"Prescott, how about giving Royce the Cook's tour?"

Once the two men left, the wet-behind-the-ears kid got to his feet and came over to stand in front of the desk, hat in hand.

James held up a hand. "One moment, Whitney." James then pointed at the office door and said to Christian, "Bring in a crew and have that door widened at least two inches on both sides."

Christian stepped up to where he could see past Whitney. "I'll have a new door milled and the stick and frame remodeled."

"And while you're at it, work on widening the aisles in the warehouse."

Christian glanced through the glass. "That's going to take considerably more time."

"True, but you'll find all the hands you need in the soup lines. We must do something to maximize the efficiency of that forklift." James faced the young man. "Okay, Whitney, what do you have for me?"

"You asked me to locate the safest banks and it turns out the safest banks are north of the border in Canada."

"Not overseas? Not the Caribbean? Why is that?"

"The Canadians have branch banking."

"What's branch banking?"

"Branch banking is, say, if a bank in Charleston had smaller banks, or branches, west of the Ashley or even on Sullivan's Island. With branch banking, you can spread the risk around."

"Spread the risk?" asked Christian, who had returned to his position next to James's desk. "But any bank can diversify their holdings, can't they?"

"They may wish to, sir, but it's difficult to diversify because small farmers are these banks' major depositors, and when small farmers can't pay their mortgage, say, because of a drop in the price of cotton, the bank fails. It's called unit banking, and a good number of states, including our own, have lobbied their state governments for unit banking—to keep the larger banks out."

Christian considered this while James asked, "So you believe we should send our money to Canada?"

"Actually I'd suggest fifty-fifty. Half would be deposited in banks such as Mellon in Pittsburgh and J.P. Morgan in New York City. They have a good number of branches."

"So," asked Christian, "we abandon the South Carolina banks and leave them to their own devices?"

"They'll fail anyway. The history of small-town banking is one of some farmer being turned down for a loan at his local bank, so he goes out and locates a financial backer and a politician to introduce the legislation."

Christian turned to James. "It doesn't seem fair. I grew up with hometown banking."

"Ah," said James with a sly smile, "and how's your hometown bank doing?"

The look on Christian's face answered that particular question.

James nodded to Whitney. "Fifty-fifty then." Until now James had never understood why he'd lost so much money investing in small, local banks, usually supported by some prominent politician. Now he understood.

Whitney turned to go.

"Wait a minute," said Christian, "if you're so smart, why are farmers doing so poorly?"

Whitney glanced at James.

His boss shrugged.

"There's way too much cotton being grown, and farmers are too stubborn to give it up. That and the fact a good number of farmers are incompetent."

"So my folks should throw in the towel?"

"If they want to make money."

"Don't be a smart-aleck."

"Christian," cautioned James, "I hired Whitney because he speaks truth to power. Don't make him feel as if his job's in jeopardy. His mother lives in the TB sanitarium in Greenville and that's not cheap."

"I'm not going to fire him, though I'd like to take him out back and kick his butt." To Whitney, he said, "My family's been dairy farmers since before the Civil War."

The young man looked at James, and again James nodded.

"But what we're considering is cotton and tobacco, and those farmers benefited from a windfall during the Great War. They've rarely made money before or since. Usually they break even, as dairy farmers do."

"Wheat, corn, cotton, and tobacco. You're saying their prices will never rise again?"

"They will when the Democrats retake the White House."

Christian turned to James, who was jotting a note on a yellow pad. "He talks like you."

James smiled. "Well, great minds . . . ."

Whitney plowed on as if not hearing this side conversation. "The government would pay your family to pour their milk in a ditch instead of taking it to market. With less product, milk prices are bound to rise."

"That's nuts! People are starving in this country."

"But less milk *will* drive up prices."

"This is crazy." Then Christian remembered that this was already happening in the milk wars in Wisconsin. His family's trucks were being stopped, their milk seized, and poured out by the side of the road. Maybe Whitney wasn't completely nuts.

"Christian, the reason I brought Whitney onboard is that I'm in the process of purchasing Royce Craven's plantations before the government starts paying farmers to plow under their crops. I want the government to pay a pretty penny for the cotton or hogs that I don't send to market."

"Then I'm your man!"

James frowned. "But what will Rachel . . . ?" James glanced at Whitney, then the yellow pad in front of him. "That will be all."

"Yes, sir."

Whitney looked at Christian, but the Wisconsinite wasn't contemplating branch banking. Christian was speculating about the satisfying nature of work. The bottom line was that he, too, needed a project.

On his way out the door, Whitney saw a copy of *The ABCs of Technocracy* lying on the wooden table.

Whitney picked up the book and faced James's desk again. "You're not reading this, are you, sir?"

"I am," said Christian. "What do you think? Could a bunch of technocrats get us out of this mess?"

"It's a bunch of hooey."

"What do you mean? There's something in the paper about technocracy every week. Important names are connected to the theory, like the economist Thorstein Veblen. A bunch of engineers just might turn the economy around."

"It's a new idea. It gives people hope." Whitney shook his head. "And it doesn't work. Have you finished reading the book?"

"Halfway through."

"When you're finished we'll talk." To James, "Someone as critical to your operation as Mister Andersen can't believe such foolishness." Whitney placed his hat on his head and opened the door. "Herbert Hoover's the world's greatest technocrat and where did that get us?"

After he left, Christian said, "That guy . . . ."

"Well, you'd best get used to working with him if you're serious about the Craven plantations."

"You believe what he says?"

"He's a Wharton School grad. Why shouldn't I?"

"But last year you said—"

"I'm a civil engineer, too, Christian. Technocracy makes perfectly good sense until, well, it doesn't." With his fountain pen James gestured at the door. "That's why I hired Whitney. I got tired of people wasting my time with pie-in-the-sky schemes. Have you ever considered how much time a person can waste trying to understand what's happening in this country? That's time and energy that should be expended in finding another way, any way, some way, to make money other than in the stock market.

"Seriously though, can you translate your dairy farming skills into making Craven's land productive? I don't need a dilettante overseeing my property."

"I'd never built a bridge before, and I certainly didn't know anything about running bootleg . . . ."

The door opened, and Prescott rolled into the room with Royce Craven behind him. For the first time Christian noticed how close the wheels of Prescott's chair came to the door framing.

"I hope I'm not interrupting," said Royce, "but I need to speak with you; you too, Christian."

James gestured at the man in the wheelchair. "We have no secrets from Prescott."

Nodding, Royce came straight to the point. "I'm sorry, James, but you're both out."

Christian looked at James. "What's he talking about?"

From his wheelchair, Prescott Mitchell leaned forward and listened intently.

"The campaign manager says having the biggest bootlegger in the state supporting the progressive platform of Leon Harris is counterproductive. I believe that's the word he used."

Remembering that Prescott and Polly Mitchell were leaving Charleston after accumulating a pile of cash from bootlegging, James looked hard at the man in the wheelchair. Prescott held up his hands in surrender and rolled back behind his table.

James looked up at Christian. "If you and Rachel were living in that house on High Battery, you'd be part of that crowd."

"But I'd still be a bootlegger."

"Would you?"

The Yankee blinked. "I'll stand by you."

"You should stand by your family. Isn't that so, Royce?"

"Well, when Prohibition ends, I doubt the boot-legger will be the most important person in a man's life."

James nodded to Christian. "Get out while the getting's good. The people south of Broad will hold you being a Yankee against you a lot longer than you being a former bootlegger."

"But what will you do?" asked Christian.

James looked at the man in the wheelchair. "I've got Prescott until Memorial Day."

"Then what? Prohibition isn't going away."

"Two more years and it's gone for good. It doesn't matter if it's Roosevelt or Smith. People want their beer back."

Royce considered this a rather bold statement, but James Stuart had a reputation for knowing his business, no matter what that business might be. James had returned from the Great War with a bunch of medals, garnered an appointment to West Point, and built a bridge over the Cooper River. Now he was running his daddy's business, and more smoothly than his father ever had. No theatrics, no confrontations, and James had recently converted an empty warehouse to a shelter for those who'd lost their homes. The Salvation Army ran that shelter now but on James's dime, and if more homeless were on their way, well, there were plenty of empty warehouses in North Charleston.

"You know," said Christian, breaking into Royce's thoughts, "I wrote a campaign check—"

"And that money will be returned to you."

"Because I'm a bootlegger or because I'm a Yankee?"

James laughed. "Take your pick."

Christian let out a long breath. "But what are we going to . . . ?"

His voice trailed off as he remembered the phone call from Jimmy Byrnes. If he hadn't been caught up in the excitement of becoming James's partner, and then the turmoil of Rachel putting the quietus on that, he would've seen this coming. They were free to promote Jim Byrnes for the United States Senate.

Confused, but about an entirely different issue, Royce asked, "Then we're still on for dinner tonight?"

"Of course," said James. "Mother expects you to call at six. Alexander will drive. And thanks for coming by and telling me personally. It couldn't have been easy. Are we still on for the old phosphate pit and that new pistol of yours?"

"Sure."

"I imagine you told Billy Ray?"

"I guess I did. Was it a secret?"

"No, but Sue Ellen never misses a chance to take

target practice, and now, I suppose, Billy Ray will join us."

"Will that be a problem?"

"Not if he's a decent shot. My sister's an excellent marksman and she takes no prisoners."

Once Royce had left, Christian turned to James. "You already knew we'd be dismissed from the Harris campaign?"

"Of course not, but I did assume the worst."

"Why didn't you tell me?"

"You know, Christian, you could learn a lot from your wife if you'd only listen. It's not yet dawned on you that the house on High Battery will open a new chapter in your life."

Christian glanced at Prescott Mitchell who was doing everything he could to make it appear that he wasn't listening.

Returning his attention to James, he found him smiling. "What? *What?*"

"Do you know how many men Rachel Belle went through to find you?"

From the table came a sudden intake of breath.

Glancing at Prescott, James said, "I don't mean what you're thinking." To his partner: "For cripes sakes, she's your wife. Would I ever talk like that about her?"

Still, Christian's tone was icy when he asked, "Just what did you mean to say?"

"That I've been forced into a great deal of contact with your wife because she loves to dance, and once she wears out her partner, she often comes looking for me. I've seen Rachel evaluate men, and within seconds dismiss them as potential mates. It drove Georgiana nuts. Then, one day you and Nicholas Eaton came into her life, and Rachel picked you. I don't think she ever completely trusted Nick." James smiled. "Anyway, you won the prize, and according to my fellow Charlestonians, you may be a damn Yankee but a Belle of Charleston chose you."

Christian stood there, stunned. He didn't know what to say. An image rushed through his mind of how taken with Rachel he had been upon first meeting her. And why not? Rachel was beautiful and charming. Every man in Wisconsin had been envious of her beauty.

James broke into his thoughts. "Remember when you were thrown out of the house during the bridge building?"

Christian remembered. He'd been drunk and tried to go upstairs where the girls had their quarters. Rachel had brained him with a cane.

"You gave Rachel a perfect chance to learn if you'd quit on her, but you didn't. You found an apartment and started to throw cocktail parties. Lots of parties."

Prescott had been listening closely. Now he said, "The Yankee Club—I remember. You and Nick were founding members."

"Nick never had a chance. By then you belonged to Rachel."

Christian shook his head. "I didn't know . . . ."

"Why don't you go home and have lunch with your wife?" James smiled as he got to his feet. "You can feel her out about running my plantations. It just might be the last building block that you two need to complete your conquest of Charleston society."

Conquest of Charleston society? How ridiculous, thought Christian. More of that south of Broad foolishness.

James smiled warmly. "It's not as foolish as you think."

What? wondered Christian.

The phone rang, James answered it, and his face lit up. "Yes, ma'am, and what can I do for you?" After the caller replied, James glanced at his watch. "Well then, I'll just have to end my day early. Mabel, I need to speak to Lewis Belle."

The operator connected James with his attorney.

"Lewis, something's come up. We'll have to discuss poll watchers at another time."

Through all this, Christian had continued to stare at James, trying to fathom what all this meant. He was a grown man with family responsibilities, a college graduate with a degree from one of the best engineering schools in the country, and on a first-name basis with most of the prominent families in Charleston, yet he had no clue as to what was expected of him.

Without another word, Christian crossed the room, took his hat from the hat rack, and left the building. All he could think of was that his wife knew more about their future than he did.

Once James had put down the receiver, Prescott asked, "Are you going to need me to stay on after Memorial Day?"

James walked to the hat rack. "Talk it over with Polly. See what she has to say."

"I know what she'll say. I can stay, but she's leaving." Grinning, he asked, "You're saying I should listen more to my wife?"

"Not at all. You're leaving Charleston, but Christian has to live here." Then, he, too, took down his hat and left the warehouse.

Outside, Alexander was waiting with the Buick and opened the back door for him. As James climbed in, he saw Christian hoofing it toward South Battery and with purpose in every step.

Alexander drove James to the marina where Hartleigh rushed into her husband's arms. Onboard the yacht James turned the engine over, Alexander cast off, and the yacht was maneuvered away from the pier. The last Alexander saw, James stood at the wheel with Hartleigh beside him, her dress billowing around her.

If James was off for the day, then he, too, was off, and it was a couple of hours before Pearl had to return to the kitchen for the evening meal. Usually, his wife napped between the noonday meal and supper, but now Alexander made other plans for her.

On the way to the house, Alexander saw Lee Randolph strolling arm and arm along the Battery with Tessa Stuart.

But hadn't Lee been holding hands with Dory Campbell just the other night? That is, until Mrs. Randolph came out on the porch and shooed Dory off to bed.

What was that white boy up to?

Alexander turned the car around and drove onto Murray Boulevard where he parked, got out, and strode onto the stone promenade. He waited there, a cloudless sky overhead, a breeze off the harbor, and Fort Sumter looming in the background. On that small island, less than three generations ago, the Union Army had held out until their flagpole had been shot down.

Did the Yankees wish to surrender? The Rebels knew the Yankees were short of men, munitions, and food. Under a flag of truce, someone representing the state of South Carolina would have to go out to Sumter and see if the Yankees wished to surrender.

Not that it would ever happen, but Alexander could've guided tours through Fort Sumter. He was a real history buff.

He took off his hat and nodded to Lee Randolph. "Sir." Then to the young man's companion, "They'd like you to return to the house, Miss Tessa."

"Why's that?" She glanced through White Point

Gardens to the house on South Battery Street.

Alexander flashed his warmest smile. "Miss Tessa, I'm just a hired hand. They don't explain these things to me." His words had the immediate effect of cutting off any challenge by Lee.

Alexander gestured at the Buick. "I have the car waiting."

Tessa looked at Lee for support, but Lee had seen a gaggle of College of Charleston girls headed in their direction.

"Well, my dear," he said, flipping his cigarette into the harbor, "I'll see you at supper."

Disappointed, Tessa reluctantly allowed Alexander to shepherd her off the promenade and down to the Buick.

At Eileen Stuart's house, Alexander and Tessa were ushered into the parlor where a bridge match was underway, a match that included Georgiana Belle. There, Alexander repeated his story.

"Thank you, Alexander. That will be all." Of Tessa, Eileen asked, "Strolling the Battery without a chaperone, were you?"

Tessa merely stood there, eyes downcast.

Georgiana cleared her throat, and once again proved that she was at the height of her game. "Eileen," she said, rising to her feet, "now that Tessa is here, I'll excuse myself."

The other two matrons remained mute. They had looked forward to an afternoon of bridge, sherry, and the latest gossip and here they were, being enlisted to discipline this child.

But they would soon have their revenge. For the rest of the afternoon, both women regaled Tessa with tales of fallen girls, victims of lost virtue.

It turned into a rather long afternoon for Tessa.

EIGHT

1931

As the political campaign picked up speed, Hartleigh and Rachel sat in the parlor one afternoon watching their children try to crawl. With Rachel's social engagements, and every hostess south of Broad unsure of whether to leave Hartleigh off the invitation list, Hartleigh had been swept up in the social scene like never before. So it was nice to have a day off, though her husband expected her to host teas for Jimmy and Maude Byrnes whenever they passed through Charleston. Hosting was the easy part; trying to understand politics was much more difficult. It was good that she had James to explain it all to her.

Of the three children, only Mary Anne could crawl. Little James crawled backwards and Jonathan Andersen just sat there.

"Jonathan," encouraged his mother from her seat, "why don't you at least give it try?"

The child stared at her, then smiled.

"Well," said Hartleigh, laughing, "what does it matter when Jonathan crawls, walks, or stands? Look at that smile. All that blond hair and the Belle blue eyes. Girls will fall all over themselves trying to please him."

"Lady-killer." Rachel forced a smile. She did not care to have her baby fall behind the development of the Stuart twins.

Hartleigh rose from her chair and went to the love seat where she picked up a bottle that had rolled under it. She passed the empty bottle to the maid, who, seeing what her mistress was doing, rushed across the room from standing near the parlor door.

"See that this gets sterilized."

"Oh, yes," said the black girl, head bobbing. "I will, I will."

"I believe we have everything in hand. You may as well return to the kitchen."

After a curtsy, the maid left the room.

Rachel said, "I really wish you wouldn't pick up after the children. It sets the wrong example for the help."

"Oh, it's no bother." Hartleigh returned to her wingback chair.

Before Rachel could further chastise her, the front door opened, slammed shut, and Dory Campbell rushed inside and stormed upstairs. That was followed by the front door reopening; then, through an open window, the young mothers heard the butler chastising the footman posted on the front porch to open the door for the master and mistress or anyone else visiting this house.

"What was that all about?" asked Rachel.

"Another broken heart, I fear."

"Haven't you spoken to Dory about Lee Randolph?"

"I've warned her that Lee appears to be the classic

rake, but she won't listen to me."

"What advice did you give her?"

"I told her to guard her heart as she would her virtue."

Rachel smirked. "And what fun would that be?"

"I'm just thankful Lee hasn't set his sights on Tessa." Hartleigh patted down the folds of her dress. "Anyway, you appear to have your work cut out for you with that new maid."

"Christian insisted we hire her. Her father can't find work. The girl's problem is that she's the apple of her father's eye and never done a lick of work."

"You don't have to justify any new hires to me. I have so many servants I have to work them in shifts."

"I've heard your mother's complaints. Hartleigh Stuart, the savior of the colored race."

"It's not my fault white people refuse to work as servants."

"No," said Rachel, chuckling, "it has to do with the attitude of white folks living south of Broad."

"That's rather blunt talk for a society matron."

"There wouldn't be any society if its matrons didn't stay the course. We've survived the Great War, the Spanish flu, and our own indulgences of the last decade. Who knows what's ahead? This recession could turn into a depression—that's what Hoover called it the other night on the radio—and then where will we be? Believe me, Hartleigh, there are more storms on the horizon, and perhaps far worse than what we've experienced. In the face of that, someone must hold fast to their moral code."

Rachel closed the book lying open in her lap. "Speaking of obligations, I need to host a twenty-fifth anniversary party for my parents, and the new house won't be ready. I wondered if—"

"Name the date," said Hartleigh with a smile. "The house is all yours. We certainly have the help."

"Well, I didn't know who to ask . . . ."

"Good idea. Why don't you ask my mother? Do you have a date in mind?"

When Rachel gave the date, Hartleigh laughed.

"Another couple who became hitched during the spring festival of flowers. Does everyone south of Broad marry in the spring?"

"Well, as you know, Charleston's summers can be a bit overwhelming."

In the hallway, the butler opened the door for Rachel's stepmother, Georgiana Belle. He took her wrap and parasol. As he did, the older woman heard the following exchange between the young mothers in the parlor:

"I take it that you're not making progress with your new sister-in-law?"

"None whatsoever and I've bent over backwards."

"You and Nell must find a way to kiss and make up, especially before this party."

"I've tried everything, but Nell won't meet me halfway."

"What does Georgiana say?"

Rachel's stepmother turned into the parlor. "I can tell you exactly what I think. You don't have to rely on my daughter's interpretation."

"Mother!" Rachel put aside *Strong Poison*, a Peter Wimsey mystery featuring the mystery writer Harriet Vane as the accused murderess. "I didn't know you were stopping by."

"I dropped by to see my grandbaby." Georgiana was fascinated with how easily this new phrase "dropped by" rolled off her tongue. Nowadays no one left cards. They simply popped in on you.

"What's this party you mentioned?" Georgiana placed her purse on an accent table and went to baby Jonathan. "There's my boy."

"Your and daddy's twenty-fifth. The house won't

be ready so Hartleigh's graciously offered to put her home at our disposal."

"The twenty-fifth," mused Hartleigh. "What's that? Silver?"

Jonathan made sputtering noises, grinned, and raised his hands for his grandmother to pick him up. Mary Anne began to cry. Little James, sucking on his pacifier, frowned.

Hartleigh left her wingback chair to console her daughter, and Little James watched, even at his young age seeming to understand that his sister was treated differently.

Georgiana asked, "And what does Elizabeth have to say about this party?" She cooed to her grandson, nestling him in the crook of her arm. "This is what life is all about. Grandchildren."

"Rachel plans to ask Mother," said Hartleigh, "but I don't see any problem there."

Georgiana had taken a seat on the love seat and began to speak baby talk to her grandson.

"Mother," said her daughter, "one of the experts writing in *Parents* magazine said you shouldn't speak baby talk to children."

Her mother harrumphed. "In my day, the family raised the children, not the federal government. The Children's Bureau," added Georgiana with an unladylike sneer, "is a bunch of overeducated ninnies who've never raised a child." She buried her face in Jonathan's tummy and blew bubbles. The baby shrieked with laughter.

"I'm sure they mean well," said Hartleigh. She put down Mary Anne, stuck a pacifier in her mouth, and returned to her seat.

"How's Nell?" asked Rachel.

"No change," said her stepmother. "I still find her in her room crying from time to time."

"Give her time," said Hartleigh. "She'll come round."

"I don't care," said Rachel rather petulantly.

"Of course you do," said her stepmother. "She's your sister-in-law. Nell's going through a rough patch. In a matter of months, her mother no longer knows her; she grows more senile everyday, and much more argumentative."

Hartleigh winced.

"I'm trying to be patient," said Rachel. "I'll be attending the Pinckneys' garden party tomorrow, but will Nell be there? She rarely is and people have noticed."

"The anniversary party is perfect for such an occasion."

Ignoring Hartleigh's suggestion, Rachel said, "One day she'll pay for her rudeness. People will cut her out. It won't matter that she's a Belle."

Georgiana returned to playing with the baby. There was no reason why her grandbaby couldn't live at the Belle mansion down the street, except for Nell Belle, nee Ingram.

"Now, Rachel," said Hartleigh, "don't be that way. Nell has lost her father, her home, and now she's losing her mother."

"And she and your brother have been married only a few months," said Georgiana. "Instead of this being a time of discovery, it's turned into a deathwatch."

"She's a disgrace to the family. I'm surprised the Laurens, the Pinckneys, or the Snowdens haven't announced a competing Memorial Day party."

Georgiana stopped bouncing the baby on her knee. "They wouldn't dare. The Memorial Day dinner is a Belle family tradition."

On Confederate Memorial Day the Belle family hosted all of Charleston, well, all the Charlestonians that mattered, by throwing a huge party. The only party rivaling the Confederate Memorial Day party was the Belle Christmas party, and no Charlestonian wanted to be left off either invitation list. After Thanksgiving Day, women checked their mail three and four times a day.

The May 6 date involved a massive buffet where hundreds of people circulated through the Belle mansion and a line ran out the front door. People came from all over. Begun shortly after the war as a display of flowers and civic pride, when the riffraff began to pollute this holy day of observance, the United Daughters of the Confederacy moved their celebration inside, but only after an afternoon of honoring the Lost Cause.

During the Gay Nineties, the Belles began to host a dinner party—invitation only—because few old line families had the money to throw such an affair. As the membership of the United Daughters of the Confederacy grew during the fraternal boom at the turn of the century, the tables disappeared, except for a few set aside for the elderly, and the buffet installed.

It was traditional to hold both the Christmas party and the Memorial Day party in the Belle ancestral home on South Battery, but Rachel Andersen wanted to change all that.

That wasn't all Rachel wanted, and much of what she wanted to see happen was coming together rather nicely. The house on High Battery that Christian had purchased had reestablished them south of Broad. She already had one baby and it was possible another was on the way, not to mention that Christian was quitting the bootlegging business.

On that particular day, Christian had asked if they could take the baby for a stroll along the Battery before Rachel left for a meeting of the Dock Street Theatre renovation group. At the turn in the rock wall that guarded the entrance to Charleston harbor, her husband paused to stare at Fort Sumter. The number of tourists visiting the site where the first shot of the Civil War was fired had markedly increased with the completion of the Cooper River Bridge, and many of those visitors came from instate.

"From the outset," said Christian, blond hair fluttering in the breeze, "I fell in love with this harbor, then you."

Holding her parasol as a shield from the sun, his wife smiled. "Are you sure it wasn't the other way round?"

"Technically speaking," said Christian, watching a ferry churn its way toward Fort Sumter, "I met you after I'd strolled the Battery."

"Technically speaking, did you say?" His wife chuckled. "This is why men have so much difficultly understanding women. My dear, it's not the women who are the problem."

Christian stared at her. James had said he should listen more to what his wife had to say. Well, he was listening, and it was like women were from another planet . . .Venus, he supposed, the planet ruling love and beauty, and if women were from Venus, men had to be from Mars.

They started off again, walking along the wall and heading in the direction of the renovated house on High Battery. "I had no idea you objected so strongly to my becoming a bootlegger."

"Are you so foolish as to think I want to be known as a bootlegger's wife?"

Rachel Belle was the end result of two hundred years of breeding in the New World; prior to that, the Belles traced their lineage all the way back to the court of Charlemagne, the founder of Europe. And though many in Charleston considered Rachel haughty—a useful pose that kept the irrelevant at bay—Rachel saw herself as the epitome of the Charleston lady:

noble, studious, religious, loving, and good. And if other women did not understand, they should either follow her lead or at least get out of her way.

And in no way did Rachel believe her marriage to a boy from Wisconsin had dimmed her hopes and dreams. During their engagement, Rachel had noticed that her fiancé was a joiner but no backslapper, that Christian never turned down any gathering she proposed they attend, or begged off a single service at the Huguenot church; not one dance, not one club, not one visitation. Not only that, but her husband might even be a clotheshorse, if that term could be applied to a man.

Still, there had been bumps along the road.

"Belles don't work for a living, Christian. At the most they're gentlemen farmers."

"I didn't like that when I first heard it, and I still don't like it. You didn't object to me working with James after his father died."

"We'd just returned from Wisconsin. I was eight months pregnant and exhausted." Rachel saw that the blanket had slipped off the baby. She bent over and tucked it around a sleeping Jonathan. "But the days of making you happy are over. It's time to think of our son's future."

"I thought I was . . . thinking of his future."

"Really? You didn't take the hint from my parents, even my brother, to use what you know at Cooper Hill, yet you come from a long line of dairy farmers."

"You made it perfectly clear that you didn't want to live in the country."

"Again, Christian, I was eight months pregnant. Of course, I didn't want to live in the country. I don't want to live there now. I'd rather live in town until Jonathan and his siblings are older. You were raised in the country, would you wish that on anyone?"

"Of course not. That's why I went to college."

"So what will you do? The house on High Battery is about finished, and I can't see you decorating it."

"Of course not. That's your responsibility, but I have had an offer I think we should consider."

NINE

When Alexander and his family went to vote—the children accompanied them to watch the adults exercise their franchise—a new clerk manned the polling place. Actually, the young man was up front flirting with Tessa Stuart and Dory Campbell, who had accompanied Elizabeth Randolph, Hartleigh Stuart, and Rachel Andersen to the polls. The men had voted before going to work, and the clerk was frankly annoyed that he actually had to do some work. He'd always heard the colored box was where you wanted to work on election day, as few Negroes ever showed up. But here they were and demanding to vote.

"Sir?" called Pearl from the rear of the building. "Sir?"

The young man stopped his flirting and reluctantly returned to the rear of the building. He did not, however, sit down, but challenged the family's right to be here.

"You sure you people should be here? This is the Democratic primary."

While Alexander stood behind his wife, hat in hand, Pearl said, "Yes, sir. We always vote the straight party ticket."

"Yeah," said Molly, "so how 'bout giving us some ballots."

Pearl hushed her sister, then returned her attention to the young man in his shiny new black suit. "Don't be offended by this fool. We're on the list. Our grandpa voted for Wade Hampton."

"I'll check the list." Lord knows why all these colored folks always said their grandpas had voted for Wade Hampton. Who the hell was Wade Hampton?

He opened the journal and checked the list as Alexander, Pearl, and Molly gave him their names and street addresses. Their names were there, so he had to assume that they could read and write and quote passages from the South Carolina constitution. Otherwise, they wouldn't be on the list.

After the polls closed, the young man asked the registrar what he was supposed to do with all the colored ballots.

"Throw them out," suggested one of the other poll workers.

"Wait a minute." The registrar knew James Stuart would be stopping by later in the evening. "Who'd they vote for?"

"Equally divided between Byrnes and Blease. A few of them for Harris."

"Then keep them," said the registrar.

* * *

"A trip to Washington? Are you out of your mind?" Elizabeth looked from Hartleigh to Sue Ellen. "It's . . . it's absurd! You're a mother now."

"All I'm asking is that you watch the children for a few days so we can attend Byrnes's swearing in."

Elizabeth Randolph crossed her arms and stared viciously at Sue Ellen. Rachel said nothing from the love seat, simply focused on her latest mystery, *The Murder at the Vicarage*, featuring Miss Marple, who until this time had been a bit player in Christie's short stories.

Glaring at Sue Ellen, Elizabeth said, "I know who put you up to this."

Sue Ellen stood shoulder to shoulder with Hartleigh. They stood so close that Elizabeth could not see Sue Ellen's hand rubbing her daughter's back for support and reassurance.

"I told you that this marriage would come to no good."

"Mother, don't be mean."

"Oh, don't worry, Mrs. Randolph," said Sue Ellen with a cherry smile. "We'll be in sleepers all the way to Washington. Lee Randolph told us all about it. The new Pullman passenger cars even have ice air-conditioning."

"Katie Stuart will take the Crescent from Greenville," added Hartleigh.

"Another Stuart. They're a plague on this house." Elizabeth sniffed. "Well, I may not be here when you return."

Rachel looked up from her mystery. *We should be so lucky.* She, however, did not comment but rose from the love seat. When she began to think such thoughts it would not be long before she expressed them. "May I be excused?" she asked.

"Certainly," said Elizabeth without giving her a second glance.

"Mother, you can always take the twins next door. Eileen said she'd be happy to watch them."

"Eileen Stuart? She's rarely home."

"Well, her year of mourning is up."

Elizabeth gave Hartleigh a sharp look. "And what does that mean? Are you suggesting that I should strut about Charleston like some trollop?"

"You never know who's out there," said Sue Ellen with yet a wider smile. "I heard through the grapevine that Royce Craven was interested in calling when you returned from the grand tour."

Elizabeth laughed out loud. "Royce Craven's definitely a gold digger, and Eileen Stuart can have him for all I care."

Sue Ellen's hand returned to stroking Hartleigh's back, and her mother returned to her rant.

"You young people are never at home. You're either down on Market Street or out on Sullivan's Island."

"It's a new world," ventured Sue Ellen, "and we're exploring it like men have done before us. The three Stuart girls are like . . . like . . . the three musketeers."

"There was a fourth if I remember," corrected Elizabeth. She crossed her arms. "Perhaps I should go along as chaperone."

"Oh, Mother," gushed Hartleigh, "I need you to take care of the twins. You know how important you are to them."

Elizabeth stood for a long moment, arms crossed and tapping her foot. She said, "Jimmy Byrnes still has to win the runoff. What if Coley Blease wins?"

Hartleigh wanted to remind her mother that Leon Harris had told his supporters to vote for Byrnes in the runoff, but half a loaf was better than none.

She threw her arms around her mother. "Oh, thank you, Mother. I knew you'd understand." After releasing her mother, Hartleigh allowed Sue Ellen to guide her out of the parlor.

"I did not dismiss you two!"

But Sue Ellen was steering Hartleigh through the double doors held open by the butler and onto the front porch.

Shaken by this encounter and unsteady on her feet, Hartleigh took her sister-in-law's arm as they went down the steps. Ahead of them, Gabriel opened the wrought-iron gate.

"Thank you, Sue Ellen. I don't think I could've done that without you." Hartleigh trembled.

In contrast, Sue Ellen beamed as they hurried for the gate. She was on her way to Washington with a couple of gal pals! No telling who they might run into on the train, and the people in the bar car were always up for a good time.

"I'm holding you and James to this trip." Sue Ellen glanced at the house as the gate closed behind them. "I know you want to get away, so is there anywhere I can drop you?"

Hartleigh considered the offer. "Let me duck into your house and make a phone call. James may be able to get away from work and meet me at the marina again."

* * *

Dory Campbell, having been abused by her father, did not put much value on personal virtue. Consequently, after an easy conquest of Dory in the shadows of the pavilion of White Point Gardens, Lee Randolph moved on to Tessa, and by the time Lee made his move, he'd already gazed deeply into Tessa's eyes, held hands with her, and occasionally kissed her—whenever he could get her alone.

Lee told Tessa that he longed to spend more time with her, his arms ached to hold her, and he bemoaned the societal rules that kept them apart.

After several days of this, and the fact that she was repeatedly told that she was the most enchanting creature to ever walk the face of the earth, well, it was enough to make Tessa forget all about Luke Andersen. So, every night when she went to bed, Tessa found herself dreaming of Lee's touch, his hand holding hers, caressing her, nibbling at her ear . . . .

Tessa's eyes popped open.

This was no dream!

A hand covered her mouth, and Lee was here—in her bed! Between her legs! And he was naked!

"Darling, it's me." Lee knew when to press his advantage, especially with anxious young schoolgirls who needed a bit of encouragement. He planted his lips on hers to awaken her desire—and to keep her mouth shut—his hands working their magic under Tessa's nightgown.

Was this really happening? How was this happening? With his mouth on hers, Tessa could not call out, but her body responded to Lee's touch—

No, no, no! It was responding to the Lee of her dreams!

Why was Lee doing this to her? Tessa didn't want to think of what might've happened if she hadn't woken up!

Unlike other girls, Tessa knew how to defend herself. She put both hands around Lee's neck and dug her thumbs in deep. When she heard something snap, she saw Lee's eyes open in surprise, felt his mouth come off hers, and his hands came out from under her nightgown. Gagging, Lee sat up, tried to right himself, but lost his balance and tumbled off the bed onto a woven rug on the hardwood floor.

After a loud thump, Tessa sat up, pushed down her nightgown, and pulled the bedsheet up around her. On the floor in the darkness, Lee thrashed around on the rug.

Should she call Doctor Rose? She'd never used her hands on a boy like that before; it'd all been an intellectual exercise.

Tessa clutched her arms around her knees and pulled them tight, and all the time Lee Randolph thrashed around on the floor beside the bed, a gurgling sound coming from him.

Tessa had been taught how to fight by her Aunt Sue Ellen. She stressed not kicking a man below the belt but jabbing a hand, fingers flat, into her attacker's throat, like a knife blade. No man expected that. A variation of that defense, if both of your hands were free, was to grasp the man's neck and squeeze, digging in with your thumbs.

"But," cautioned Sue Ellen, "if slapping a man— always a girl's first line of defense—fails, then go for the throat or stomp on his instep, especially if your arms are locked down at your sides or held over your head." Sue Ellen had had her practice these moves over and over again. "Practice makes perfect."

In the darkness, Lee Randolph was quiet. He didn't move.

Was he unconscious?

"Lee?"

No answer.

"Lee! Speak to me! No games, please."

A knock at the door.

"Miss Tessa?" The upstairs maid cracked the door and light spilled in from the hallway. "You alright?"

"Bad dream."

"Well, if you need anything—"

"I'll be sure to call."

"You don't need me to sleep at the foot of your bed the rest of the night?"

Tessa glanced at the body beside the bed. "No thank you."

Once the door shut, Tessa dropped the sheet,

then made sure her nightgown was settled properly on her shoulders and below her knees. Tentatively, she stepped down from the bed, an antique four-poster monster that sat unusually high off the floor. One foot came down on a piece of clothing, the other on a shoe, almost turning her ankle.

Tessa jerked her foot back.

"Lee?" she asked in a hoarse whisper.

No answer.

Tessa pulled up her legs, rolled to the opposite side of the bed, and slipped off. As she rounded the foot of the bed, she snatched her robe off her hope chest. Slipping into the robe, she said, "Lee, please answer me."

He did not.

Tessa hiked up her garment and dropped to her knees beside him. Could Lee have fainted? "Lee?"

He remained silent as did the whole household.

She reached for the lamp on her nightstand—and almost knocked it over. Springing to her feet, she grabbed the neck and righted the lamp. She glanced at the clock.

Just past three. She'd never been up this late, even at slumber parties.

"Lee?"

She'd have to touch him. Shake him awake.

Impossible! He was naked.

Tessa leaned back against the bed, shoulders slumped. Had she killed him? Was that even possible? Any moment she expected Lee to leap to his feet and shout, "Aha!"

Lee had been so sweet and kind. How could he have been so reckless with her honor? No gentleman would've handled her virtue in such a careless manner. Perhaps he'd been drunk.

That had to be it!

But if Lee wasn't drunk, then she meant nothing

more to him than any other loose girl.

Why did this always happen to her? Last year, she and Luke had been caught skinny dipping by a group of rumrunners on the Isle of Palms. That time Uncle James had buried the story in a lie so simple that it had actually worked. Now she would need another lie.

Tessa stared at the form with a growing sense of panic. Her hands began to tremble. She might soil her panties if she continued to sit there and do nothing.

Those willing are able.

The Ashley Hall motto.

Those willing are able, or as one wag had said: *If it's to be, it's up to me.*

Tessa glanced at the window, its curtains rustling in a breeze.

TEN

The following morning, the butler for Eileen Stuart—another rock in any storm—found Alexander smoking a cigarette and drinking coffee on the porch of the carriage house.

The butler waved at him.

"What you doing up so early?" asked Alexander, looking through the balusters.

"I value your opinion on a matter."

Alexander motioned the butler up to where he sat on the narrow porch.

"I don't think so. I think you should come down here."

James was on his way to breakfast when he realized something was amiss. Passing the red tips separating his house from his mother's, he saw two Negroes staring at a pile of clothing.

What's this?

James pushed his way through his mother's wrought-iron gate and walked around the side of the house where the two Negroes stood. Behind him, the wrought-iron fence creaked close.

Good Lord, it's young Randolph!

"What happened?"

"The yardman found him this way," said the butler.

Looking around, James realized the yardman was nowhere to be found.

"Dead," confirmed Alexander.

The three of them looked up the side of the house, following the main vent stack for the upstairs and downstairs bathrooms.

"Whose room is that?"

"Miss Tessa's."

James's father had eschewed modern conveniences, but the day after his father's funeral, James's mother informed her son that she wanted the plumbing renovations to commence the following week. James remembered that as the day his mother finally stepped out of his father's shadow.

"Obviously young Randolph fell off this stink pipe," said James, "which begs the question: was he coming or going?"

Neither black man cared to speculate.

James asked the butler to inform his mother that he would be late for their breakfast, and the butler left to do so.

"And oil that gate!" he called after him.

"Yes, sir, I will inform the yardman of that matter."

"What do you think?" James asked Alexander.

"That this is one foolish white boy."

"Why do you say that?"

"Why didn't he take off his shoes? It certainly would've made it easier climbing that pipe, no matter whether he was coming or going."

James knelt beside the dead man. Seeing no other injuries, he pulled down the collar and felt the throat. The larynx gave way. Lee must've died of asphyxia when his trachea collapsed.

"Isn't that how we teach our women to protect themselves?" asked Alexander.

James rose to his feet. "But I've never seen the results."

"Pearl used it one time, and this is how I found the body. The throat collapses."

"I never considered the outcome."

"Because men don't fight this way."

Both men stared at the window again, then James looked behind him at the row of red tips.

"I think what happened is this boy died when he fell over the wrought-iron fence on *my* property. Get him through that passage in the red tips, the one we used as kids."

Alexander bent over and scooped up the dead man. "And Doctor Rose?"

"I'll phone him."

"Should young Randolph be found lying across the fence?"

"Your call, but he should be drunk. I'll bring along the whiskey."

By the time James had returned next door, Alexander was pushing his way through the red tips behind the wrought-iron fence separating James's front yard from its rear.

The footman heard the gate squeak next door and flipped his cigarette into the street. After leaving open his own gate, Gabriel sprinted ahead of James and opened the front door, then the interior one. At this time of the morning the butler was occupied serving breakfast.

"This place is about to get very busy, Gabriel, so stay on your toes."

Puzzled, the footman said, "Yes, sir."

In his study, James asked Mabel to put through a call to Doctor Rose. James told Rose that there had been an accident.

"Who's hung over from last night?" demanded the doctor.

James paused.

The operator said, "I won't say a word."

Annoyed, James spit out, "Lee Randolph."

Rose and James heard a sudden intake of breath on the line.

"You coming or not?" asked James.

"I'll be right there."

They disconnected, then James went to the wet bar where he took out a bottle of whiskey.

His mother-in-law saw the bottle as he left the study. "Drinking this early in the day? Not a good sign, James."

"Trust me, Mother, this will be a difficult day for everyone."

James found Randolph's body lying in a heap on the far side of the wrought-iron fence separating the front yard from its rear.

"Trying to revive him," explained Alexander, "I pulled him off the fence." The black man gestured at the young man's throat. "But there's still rust there."

"Gotcha." James handed the bottle across the fence. "Nail that down next door."

Eyeing the contents, Alexander said, "This is pretty good whiskey. Sure you want to use it?"

"Always go first class when you're selling a lie."

Alexander chuckled. "Spoken like a true rich man." He twisted the lid off the bottle and downed the liquor, then became aware of Gabriel gaping at them from the wraparound porch.

To him Alexander said, "You'll lose your job if we

learn you're not trustworthy, and jobs are hard to come by these days, especially for colored boys."

"Yes, sir." Gabriel nodded rapidly. *"Yes, sir!"*

"Doctor Rose?" asked Alexander as he sprinkled liquor on the dead man's chest.

"On the way."

Alexander poured the remainder of the whiskey into Lee's mouth where it immediately pooled up. Alexander pushed down on the dead man's throat and the small pool of whiskey disappeared down Lee's throat.

He looked at James. "The law?"

"Let Rose notify them. Post Gabriel at the gate with orders not to allow anyone back here except Rose and the beat cop."

Again Alexander glared at the porch where the boy continued to gape at them. "You get that, boy?"

"Yes, sir!" And Gabriel left the porch to guard the gate at the sidewalk.

Returning to the house, James found Elizabeth drinking coffee and speculating on her son-in-law's use of the word "Mother." James knelt before her as she sat in the love seat and he took her hands in his.

"What's this, James?" asked Elizabeth, amused.

"Get a grip, Mother. Lee Randolph's body has just been found in our side yard. It appears he fell across the wrought-iron fence and broke his neck."

"My God!" Elizabeth's hands slipped from his and rose to her throat. "What will I tell his family?"

"They shouldn't be surprised. Lee Randolph was much too reckless for his own good." James stood up. "Inform everyone in this house. I'll do the same at my mother's."

"Should I come outside?" asked Elizabeth.

"It's nothing a lady should be subjected to."

"Yes, yes, thank you. I think I'll go upstairs now."

Taking her arm, James escorted his mother-in-law from the parlor.

At the foot of the stairs, he asked, "Sure you're up to this? I can accompany you."

Elizabeth nodded. "Thank you."

Christian came up the hallway from breakfast.

"Wait right here, Mother."

James took Christian aside and explained what had happened as Elizabeth waited at the foot of the stairs. "Could you give Mother a hand upstairs?"

"Of course." He glanced at Elizabeth. "You know," said the Yankee, "I don't believe I mentioned this, but I've come home and found Lee walking on the porch railing to impress the girls."

Hearing this, Elizabeth said from the stairs, "I'll inform Dory. She had a terrible crush on Lee."

"And I'll break the news to Rachel."

"Don't worry, Christian, I can tell her."

"No, ma'am," he said, taking her arm. "I should be the one to tell my wife."

They went upstairs.

Outside, the beat cop stood beside Rose as the physician examined the body.

"Officer," said James, "feel free to use our phone if you don't care to broadcast this over your radio."

The beat cop nodded. Ordinary folks were always on the lookout for any reason to wander through a house south of Broad. The cop would definitely take James up on his offer.

Outside the fence, a crowd had begun to gather.

And why not? thought James. Charleston used to hold mass hangings of pirates just down the street at White Point Gardens.

Opening the door to his mother's house was the butler who had found Lee's body.

"Check with Alexander before you go spreading any gossip."

The butler nodded. "Yes, sir."

James went upstairs to his mother's bedroom. After tapping on the door and announcing himself, James let himself in.

"Oh, there you are," said his mother, smiling. She was already dressed for the day and wore rather cheerful attire. That was all about to change.

James took his mother's hand and led her over to a settee. He sat down, put an arm around her, and explained what had happened to Lee Randolph.

"Oh, my lord!" said Eileen, straightening up on the settee and slipping out of his arms.

James rose to his feet. "I'll tell Tessa, but give me a few minutes. She had a crush on the boy."

"Oh, Lordy," moaned his mother from the settee.

"You might want to tell Sue Ellen."

While his mother sat there, shoulders slumped and wondering what her obligations were to the dead man's family, James left the room, crossed the hallway, and knocked on Tessa's door.

No answer.

He knocked again, this time a good bit harder.

The upstairs maid spoke from an alcove where she served morning coffee and hot biscuits. "Tessa didn't sleep well last night, Mister James."

He knocked again, this time more vigorously.

"Yes? What is it?" The girl's voice was full of sleep.

"It's Uncle James. I'm coming in. Make yourself decent."

James waited a couple of beats, then opened the door and crossed the room. As he did, he examined the floor.

Nothing there. No blood, no urine, no nothing. Had anything actually happened in here last night? He glanced at the window. It was closed.

"What?" Tessa sat in her bed with the bedcovers pulled around her. "What's wrong, Uncle James?"

He took a seat on the edge of the bed. "Tessa, you need to brace yourself for some very bad news."

The girl's eyes shone with fear. "Er . . . what do you know?"

Because of her reply, James knew how to play this. "Lee Randolph has been found lying across the wrought-iron fence on the other side of the red tips. Not in this yard, but in the yard next door. My yard. It would appear Lee got drunk, tried to walk the porch railings—you and Dory have seen him do this before—and he fell off. Lee's dead."

Tessa did not shriek or express dismay. She did, however, begin to cry and lean into him. When the sheet fell away James took her into his arms. "Tessa, you're not in any trouble."

He waited until she could control her weeping. When Tessa pushed away, she was wiping away the tears. She tried to say something, but James put a finger to her lips and pulled up the sheet. Tessa tightened it around her again.

He glanced at the door. "Listen, and listen fast. All you need to know is that Lee Randolph's body was found in my yard where he evidently landed on the fence, crushing his larynx. Under no circumstances are you to take the blame for his death."

Tessa stared at her uncle, mouth open, then leaned into him again. "I'm sorry," she said over his shoulder. She hugged him. "I did what Aunt Sue Ellen taught me."

"And I'm proud of you. What you did last night honored this house."

Leaning back, she regarded him. "Really?"

"When you tell a gentleman to stop, he should stop. Lee Randolph was no gentleman, and I under-stand what you had to do. I'm not so excited about the fact that you may have had to dress him, but I don't want to know about that."

Tessa lowered her eyes. "You've had to do this before."

James smiled reassuringly. "What else would a father do for his child?"

Her head came up. "But I'm your niece."

"Soon you'll be more than that. Lewis Belle has the paperwork your father signed in the event I should have to adopt you. In a few days, you'll be my daughter." He smiled. "Now, how would you like to go to Chicago to see Luke Andersen? There's a convention coming up, then a world's fair."

"Really?" Tessa broke into a huge smile. "Oh, Uncle James, that would be marvelous." She threw her arms around him and hugged him tight. Uncle James was the one person she could count on. No wonder Hartleigh loved him so.

Over her shoulder, he said, "Tessa, I can't take you to Chicago unless you're my ward."

Nodding, Tessa leaned back again. "Whatever you say." Tears ran down her cheeks. She was finally home. She was safe. She dabbed at the tears.

"I need you to be involved in this runoff election. Byrnes is your ticket to Chicago."

"Of course. Whatever you want me to do."

"If you do as I ask, Hartleigh and I will take you to Chicago. No twins, and certainly no Dory."

"But why—"

"Think about it. Didn't Dory accompany Mrs. Randolph on her grand tour of Europe?"

"Yes . . . ."

"Don't you deserve such a trip?"

Tessa didn't know how to respond. She simply smiled.

"I know this is heresy in this town, but there's more to the world than Charleston."

Tessa picked at the bedsheet. "If I were a boy, I wouldn't be in all this trouble. I'd be on my father's boat."

"But you wouldn't be so dadgum pretty." He smiled broadly.

Tessa beamed until there was a knock at the door, then her face filled with anxiety.

James gripped Tessa's arms and looked her in the eye. "You're to follow my instructions to the letter. You go against me and no trip. Got it?"

Tessa set her jaw. "Got it."

"And you're to have a good breakfast and dress for school. It's going to be a very long day."

James stood up as his mother and the upstairs maid entered the room. Eileen Stuart went straight to her grandchild and took James's place on the bed.

Hugging the teenager, she said, "Tessa, darling, I'm so sorry. Lee was a wonderful young man."

Tessa looked over her grandmother's shoulder at her uncle.

"She doesn't want to talk about it, Mother. She needs to get ready for school."

"But this morning of all mornings—"

"I know people will want to discuss this ad nauseam, but there's no advantage in that for Tessa."

"James," said his mother, releasing the girl, "a young man has died, tragically."

"But must his death be blown all out of proportion?"

"James, that's not—"

He pulled his mother to her feet, put his arm around her, and walked her out of the room, leaving the maid with his niece.

In the hallway, he said, "Lee was nothing to her, well, nothing more than a competition between two teenage girls, but by the time Charleston gets through with this, Lee will be the love of Tessa's life or they'll be star-crossed lovers, or worse, his death was the result of a love triangle involving she, Lee, and Dory Campbell."

"Aren't you being a bit melodramatic?"

Knowing his mother would never agree unless he quoted a higher authority, James added, "Hartleigh explained this to me, and since I'm the responsible party, I simply extrapolated."

"Well, I don't know . . . ."

"Please, Mother. Dory's being boosted by everyone, but no one's supporting Tessa."

Eileen started to object, but her son raised a finger. "Prescott and Polly are returning to Missouri, you're being courted by Royce Craven, and Sue Ellen spends her nights down on Market Street or out on Sullivan's Island, so who does that leave for Tessa?"

"I'd . . . I'd never thought of it that way."

"Tessa's my ward—the paperwork is being processed as we speak—and I'll protect her from everyone, even you."

"James, you know I'd never—"

He put a finger to her mouth. "Please, Mother, can't we consider Tessa's future and not her past?"

"Well, of course."

"Then help the girl. Make these people go away."

"What people?"

At that moment, Sue Ellen came tearing out of her bedroom while pulling on her robe; below them, Polly Mitchell started up the stairs, and through the front door rushed Hartleigh, all intent on comforting the poor girl who had just lost her boyfriend.

James smiled. "What people indeed."

ELEVEN

When James returned to his house, the body was gone, the crowd had been dispersed, and Alexander was shoving a push mower around both sides of the wrought-iron fence. James saw Gabriel posted at the gate and a houseboy stationed at the front door. When he entered the house, he found everyone in the parlor. He motioned for Christian to join him in the hallway.

"Can you take Rachel upstairs?"

Christian did.

Entering the parlor, James said, "Dory, could you wait upstairs? Mrs. Randolph and I have a great deal to discuss."

Dory looked at her mentor.

Elizabeth said, "This may not be the best time, James."

"But Dory has school today."

"Oh, James, don't be so heartless."

Opening his hands wide, palms out, he asked the runaway, "Would you rather stay here or go somewhere else? We discussed whether you wanted to return to your father's farm or remain with Mrs. Randolph and attend Ashley Hall."

"Summerville?" cut in Elizabeth. "Now why in the world would the child want to return to Summerville?"

But Dory had already leaped to her feet. "I'll get ready for school." And she disappeared upstairs.

"James, what's going on?"

"Mother, you and Dory are guests in my home, not permanent residents."

Elizabeth straightened up. "Now, why in the world would you say something like that?"

"If the chief of police okays it, Randolph's body will be on a train bound for Richmond tonight. What happened last night was tragic, but Lee belongs in Richmond, not Charleston."

"Not even a memorial service?"

Christian trotted downstairs and turned into the parlor. "Anything I can do?"

"Well, Alexander's tidying the yard. He'll soon be available to move the body from the morgue to the train station."

James addressed the butler, who had quit the dining room to attend to his duties at the door. "Have one of the maids pack Randolph's clothing and have his luggage brought downstairs. Leave it at the front door until you hear from Alexander. You're responsible for that luggage and its contents."

"Yes, sir."

"James, usually I—"

Her son-in-law held up his hand. "Not now, Mother." To Christian: "Once the chief of police okays it, Randolph's body will be shipped to Richmond. I'm insisting that it go tonight since they have the whole day for the autopsy, but someone needs to accompany the body to the train station." He glanced at his mother-in-law on the love seat. "It'll make the women feel so much better if a servant is with the body while at the train station. Alexander can escort the body back to Richmond."

"I can handle that," said Christian, who had never liked Lee. "We'll use one of the trucks to move the body from the coroner's office to Union Station."

"James—"

"Mother, don't concern yourself with this. I've spoken with Lewis Belle, who's put the paperwork in motion for me to become Tessa's legal guardian. I insisted my brother leave this paperwork with Lewis years ago. Then there's the matter of Dory Campbell. When Tessa moves in, Dory will be out of a room."

"Out of a room!" Elizabeth rose from the love seat.

"Mother, try to understand. Any child under my protection will not live next door, not at this point in her life."

"But poor Dory—"

"Poor Dory has been boosted long enough. It's time for Tessa to have some boosters. You're welcome to live here, but you should always feel free to find other accommodations. Dory can even sleep in your room."

"But my maid sleeps at the foot of my bed."

"I'll leave that to you, but Dory must never be led to think she's more than a guest in this house."

His mother-in-law opened her mouth, then shut it.

"Now," said James to Christian, "let's have breakfast and divvy up the chores." Before he left the parlor, James said, "Send Dory over to my mother's when she's ready for school." He glanced at his wristwatch. "Christian, could you head over to Mother's and restart breakfast?"

"Got it!" said Christian with more enthusiasm than necessary. Life was again in motion.

After the Yankee left, James said to his mother-in-law, "Tessa and Dory don't need any more drama. And the girls are not to be encouraged to make of this any more than what Lee Randolph was: a rake passing through and collecting scalps."

"But all I wanted—"

"Was to embellish this incident so you'd become more important than you actually are in this narrative."

"Why, I never!" Her hands went to her hips.

"Secure a suite at the Charleston Hotel. I'll cover all expenses." At the parlor door, James faced her again. "And, Elizabeth, if you do go, make sure you take that brat with you."

On his way over to his mother's, he ran into his wife.

Hartleigh had been crying. "Oh, James, isn't it terrible?"

"It's worse than that."

"What?" She dabbed at her eyes. "What do you mean?"

"Your mother's undermining my authority and I may have to ask her to move out. Why don't you talk some sense into her?"

A half hour later, James escorted the girls into Ashley Hall where he asked for a quick word with Miss McBee.

Mary Vardrine McBee knew the Stuart family from their donations to both the school and the new public library. The only all-girl college-preparatory school in the state, Ashley Hall graduates often went on to the College of Charleston, but just as many attended one of the Seven Sisters, the all-girls' schools north of the Mason-Dixon Line.

Sitting across from the headmistress, James

said, "You, of course, have heard of the incident this morning at my house."

Charleston's first radio station, WCSC, had just gone on the air broadcasting from the Francis Marion Hotel, and its staff cast around for anything to broadcast: news, sports, weather—and gossip. The station couldn't stop talking about the odd manner of Lee Randolph's death.

"If I may, I'd like to point out that Lee Randolph was not invited into my home. That was the doing of my mother-in-law, but once he arrived I set the Pinkertons on him."

Miss McBee blinked. Now that was different.

"Turns out Mister Randolph left Richmond with a couple of husbands in hot pursuit."

A small gasp from McBee.

"Once Randolph arrived, he preyed on two naive teenagers and set them to quarreling over him. Now, I believe a young lady's education is much more important than it has been in the past and I will not allow these girls to be distracted from their schoolwork. That's why they came to school today. As for my niece, the paperwork has been set in motion for Tessa to become my ward. My wife, also one of your graduates, will supervise Tessa, and wherever we go, Tessa will also go."

"So you're leaving Charleston, Captain Stuart?"

"Actually, that reference is to the Mann Act."

McBee nodded, unsure of where this conversation was going.

"The Democratic convention will be held in Chicago, and I promised Tessa I'd take her there."

"I didn't know Tessa was that interested in politics."

"Oh," said James, smiling, "I doubt she is, but that's the angle she's working. My partner's brother is on scholarship at the University of Chicago. They dated when Luke was here last year."

McBee smiled. "And you negotiated her good conduct for a trip to Chicago."

"Which she completely forgot about once she was under the spell of Lee Randolph."

McBee leaned into her desk. "Leave this to me, Captain Stuart. We're used to working with lovesick girls who need to be distracted."

Georgiana found her daughter-in-law in the upstairs parlor. The upstairs parlor had been converted from the least of the bedrooms when the upstairs reception room had been moved downstairs and the former upstairs reception room had been converted into two separate bedrooms with all the modern-day conveniences, including walk-in closets and full baths. In this conversion yet another piece of Belle family lore was lost as the upstairs reception room had been called the "twins' room," named for Alexis and Jennie Belle, sisters who'd held their coming-out balls there, that is, until the Yankees put an end to that way of life.

Nell looked up from where she sat in one of the upholstered mahogany chairs at a heavy wooden circular table with a Tiffany lamp overhead. In front of her lay an open Bible.

"Mrs. Belle!" Nell scrambled to her feet.

"Perhaps it's time for you to call me 'Mother,' or at least, 'Georgiana.'" She joined her daughter-in-law at the table, taking the empty chair across from her. A houseboy scooted the chair under her.

Her personal maid had accompanied her into the room, and Georgiana asked for two glasses of sherry.

While the maid poured the sherry at a small bar that folded into itself, Georgiana made herself comfortable and Nell tucked loose strands of hair behind her ears. When the sherry arrived, Nell accepted the glass with a forced smile.

Georgiana asked the maid if she'd like to take a glass with her when she returned to her post outside the door.

"Yes, ma'am." The maid poured glasses of sherry for herself and the houseboy, cutting the sherry with water for the boy. Both servants thanked their mistress and left the room, closing the door behind them.

"The only way to keep the servants out of the sherry is to not put it completely off limits." Georgiana sipped from her glass.

Again, Nell flushed. She'd been into the sherry quite a bit lately and hoped it would be blamed on some unknown servant.

Georgiana put down her glass. "Did I tell you that my family lost everything in the crash of ninety-three?"

Nell shook her head.

"Like the Belles, we had a rice plantation, though ours was in Georgetown County."

"My father was from Georgetown."

"Yes, yes," said Georgiana with a genuine lack of interest. "My family survived the war, the Yankee invasion, and the Great Depression, only to be trip-ped up by the crash in 1893."

"The Great Depression?"

"The panic of '73 caused by the fall of the price of silver. That depression lasted so long that people began to call it the Great Depression." Georgiana picked up her sherry glass. "My goodness, Nell, when you have the opportunity to attend a good boys' school, such as the College of Charleston, make the most of it."

Georgiana took another sip from her glass. Perhaps she'd gone too far. No. That wasn't true. Rachel was ready to debut her new home. Interior decorators were working night and day, and Nell's intransigence could no longer be tolerated.

"Well," said her daughter-in-law, "history was never my strong suit."

"And you live in Charleston—no, no." Georgiana waved off any protests. "I remember what it was like to be young. Life begins when boys take an interest in you, and after that there's no advantage in revealing the extent of your education. I'll have volume one of Yates Snowden's *History of South Carolina* sent to your room."

"Volume one?"

"No reason for the other four volumes to languish on your bookshelf until you've shown a bit of interest in the subject."

Georgiana sipped sherry while Nell pondered her fate.

A five-volume set? My goodness, I may as well be studying for the bar.

"Since our current circumstances bring back memories of previous recessions, it might be good for you to remember Jennie Belle's maxim: the next calamity is straight ahead, so pay off your debts and always keep some money under the mattress."

"I . . . I never heard that before, but it does make sense."

"Jennie Belle was the cleverest woman the Belle family produced since Catherine Belle."

"Catherine? I don't know that I've heard that name."

"She's the one who reestablished the Belle line in the New World, and she married her cousin so there would be no question regarding the bloodline. You might remember that when it comes to naming your second daughter."

"My second daughter?"

"Well," said Georgiana with a warm smile, "your

mother might not remember you, but you'll want your family remembered."

Nell returned the smile. "Thank you."

"Don't worry. There's plenty of time to change your mind."

"Change my mind about what?" Just when she thought she'd gotten a grasp on the conversation . . . .

"Whether you name your first child Jennie or Catherine."

"Oh," said Nell, smiling, "that was a joke."

Georgiana arched an eyebrow. "With some distance from your recent tragedies, you may simply wish to call your firstborn child 'Ingram.' Now, why don't we have lunch sent up?"

"Lunch?"

"Isn't that what you young people call the midday meal? You don't have much use for 'luncheon.' It sounds much too formal."

Nell laughed. "Oh, Mrs. Belle, you sound so hip."

"Hip?" asked the older woman.

The heavy circular table was set with a tablecloth and cloth napkins and plenty of silverware, two glasses of sweet tea, and the appropriate condiments. Two gherkin pickles flanked a pile of chicken salad on a bed of lettuce. Once Nell said the blessing and their meal was underway, Georgiana continued her daughter-in-law's education.

"There are many important families in this city, and every generation produces the next great lady who comes to dominate Charleston society. In your generation, it's my stepdaughter."

"Rachel?" Nell laughed. "Pardon me, but how can that be? She's no longer a Belle."

Georgiana cut her eyes toward the servants. "Did I ever tell you how my husband swept me off my feet to Charleston?"

Nell didn't hear a word. She was caught up in a whirlwind of emotions. Rachel Andersen was the next great society dame?

Impossible! She'd married a Yankee! Actually, Rachel had spent the first months of her marriage in Wisconsin.

Dairyland, Wisconsin! And now she'd been reduced to living with that awful Elizabeth Randolph.

Except that Rachel's husband had purchased her family home on High Battery! It was being renovated as they spoke. No telling what changes Rachel had made in her home . . . .

Her mother-in-law came back into focus.

What was the old woman saying? Something about the Belle family . . . that was all they talked about in this house . . . the Belles . . . the Belles of Charleston . . . there must be more important families.

"I said name one," said Georgiana.

"What?" Nell came out of her fog. Was the old woman a mind reader?

"You look as I did when I learned Cousin Mary had engineered the marriage that brought me into the fold." Georgiana returned to her chicken salad. After chewing a bite, she added, "It was a compliment, but I didn't realize it at the time. To outsiders, the idea of one family dominating Charleston society sounds preposterous, but name one girl in your generation who's been so dominant?

"Who was class president of Ashley Hall, president of her sorority, and vice president of the College of Charleston? And at the C of C, Rachel had to play second fiddle to some young man." Georgiana smiled. "If you had to name the queen bee of your generation—the one young lady who belongs to all the correct clubs and organizations—who would that be?"

Nell hadn't thought about it, but the answer to all

those questions was Rachel Belle Andersen.

"And who's best at all these silly dances your generation has embraced: the Charleston, the Black Bottom, and the Lindy Hoop."

"Hop. The Lindy Hop."

Georgiana returned to her chicken salad. "And you must be at the latest hot spot." She looked up. "Isn't that the correct word? Your generation has so many new words and phrases that my generation has become quite confused."

"Actually, nightclubs have given way to dance marathons."

"Does Rachel participate?"

"Poor Christian . . . it's difficult." Nell stopped. There wasn't any social activity in which Rachel didn't excel. Sometimes Rachel paired up with James Stuart, who appeared to have unlimited energy. James certainly liked to cut a rug.

"Rachel would like to host the Memorial Day dinner."

"Here? At your house?"

"Actually, at your former home, but she can wait."

"Wait for what?"

"For your understanding."

"Understanding? Understanding what?"

"Isn't that what we've been discussing, your understanding of how the Belle family works? My stepdaughter serves on so many boards, so many charities, and even counsels the minister at the Huguenot church. I don't know how she keeps up."

"Franklin and I attend the Presbyterian church."

"The Presbyterians have too many freethinkers. Someone must bring order to Charleston and we Huguenots do that."

"But Franklin enjoys worshipping there. You've heard him go on at length . . . at your Sunday luncheons after services."

Georgiana didn't reply, only munched on a gherkin. Nell realized the Belle family wanted this to be her decision. Or she could continue to stall. And how would that look to those living south of Broad?

Later in the day, Nell called her sister-in-law. "Rachel, would you have time to show me the changes you've made in my house? I didn't want to intrude while you were having the work done. It is, after all, your home now."

"Oh, Nell," gushed Rachel, "I've been hoping you'd call. Can we do it tomorrow morning? I'm hosting my bridge club this afternoon." Rachel paused. "You must join us one afternoon."

Nell could not believe what she was hearing. Rachel sounded as if she was thrilled to hear from her.

Hmm, guess I've signed up to play second fiddle to Rachel Andersen, nee Belle.

At the Stuarts', Rachel returned the handset to its cradle in the upstairs hallway and motioned her maid to join her in her bedroom. After Gladys closed the door, Rachel gestured at the mysteries stacked by her bed.

"Get rid of these books. We're back in business."

A smile appeared on the Negro's face and she clapped her hands. "Oh, goody, Mrs. Andersen. I'll fetch a houseboy." Gladys turned to go.

"And, Gladys . . . ."

The Negro faced Rachel again. "Yes, ma'am."

"When we're alone, feel free to call me Miss Belle."

* * *

The thermometer showed one hundred and five degrees when the Pinkerton agent finally tracked down Sue Ellen's husband. Fans whirled overhead and people commented that it was only a dry heat. Still, everyone sweated.

The Pinkerton extended a hand across the desk. "Telegram, sir, if you're Edmund Hall."

"I am."

Edmund took the envelope and ripped it open. He was one of many engineers sitting at desks in a hastily built building, one of the first in Boulder City. And though he'd participated in building the bridge over the Cooper River and the Empire State Building, Edmund worked as a common draftsman, as did all the other young men in the room. But he did have a job.

The Pinkerton did not leave, but Edmund failed to notice this until he finished reading the telegram.

My dear Edmund. STOP. Your mother did not wish to worry you. STOP. In declining health. STOP. I return to Charleston tomorrow. STOP. Round trip ticket enclosed. STOP. Love Sue Ellen.

His mother was ill? First he'd heard of it, and he received a letter every month, several pages of gossip about the goings-on in Raleigh. He should've insisted that his mother install a telephone.

Another envelope was handed to him.

Edmund ripped this one open, too. Inside was a train ticket and five twenty-dollar bills.

Edmund was on the next train east. In Atlanta, he added a stopover in Charleston. Though Charleston was well out of the way, Edmund knew if he didn't stop on the way to Raleigh, he wouldn't have the nerve to stop on the return trip to Vegas.

In Charleston he took a taxi to the house on South Broad where he pushed through the gate—it squeaked—and found his wife sitting on the front-porch swing with Billy Ray Craven.

TWELVE

Sue Ellen leaped from the swing. "What are you doing here?"

Hauling his suitcase up on the porch, her husband said, "Oh, it's not 'good to see you' or 'what a surprise' or 'thank goodness you're home,' but 'what are you doing here?'"

Billy Ray joined her, saying something silly about Sue Ellen becoming his sister.

Edmund decked him.

Sue Ellen screamed, and when Billy Ray struggled to his feet, Sue Ellen tried to go to him.

"No!" Edmund had dropped his suitcase. Now he grabbed his wife's arm and pulled her away.

"But he's hurt."

Billy Ray heaved himself to his feet using the porch railing.

"I'll hit him again if he ever touches you."

While Edmund was speaking to Sue Ellen, Billy Ray hit him upside the head. Again Sue Ellen screamed, and Edmund, a Golden Gloves boxer, stumbled back and sat down hard.

Billy Ray took his handkerchief from a pocket and dabbed at his busted lip. "You forget yourself, Edmund. This is my town."

The engineer leaped to his feet. "And this is *my* woman." Without looking at Sue Ellen, he added, "Get inside."

"Edmund . . . ."

His fists came up. "Get inside! Now!"

When her husband looked her way, Billy Ray hit him again, and Edmund staggered back, losing his balance at the edge of the porch, stumbling down the steps, and sitting down hard, this time in the grass.

Deciding discretion was the greater part of valor, Sue Ellen disappeared inside her house and cowered behind the door.

Prescott Mitchell rolled out of his bedroom, the former study of Sue Ellen's father. "What's the racket?" Draped across his lap and legs was a blanket. His shirt was a pajama top.

"Billy Ray and Edmund are fighting."

Prescott looked at Sue Ellen with disgust. "Uh-huh, and we know who's to blame for that."

Sue Ellen held open the door and Prescott rolled onto the porch. There he saw the two men on the lawn punching away, Edmund scoring points with his technique, but wary of a blow from the larger man, who could easily put him on the ground again.

"Hey!" shouted Prescott. "Cut it out!"

Neither man paid the least bit of attention: Edmund, a focused Golden Gloves trained boxer and Billy Ray, an experienced brawler. Inside the house, Sue Ellen peered out a window. Boys hadn't fought over her since her days at the College of Charleston.

"Hey!" tried Prescott again. "I said stop it!"

No response. Edmund and Billy Ray continued to circle each other, watching for an opening.

Prescott pulled a pistol from under his lap blanket and fired a warning shot over the Ashley. Both men glanced in his direction, and it was not lost on Prescott that neither man's hands came down and both took a step back. Up the street came the wail of a siren, lights came on along South Battery, and a window was raised here and there. Heads stuck out of those windows.

"It's over! Go home to your wives."

Neither moved, nor did their fists come down.

"Listen up! There's a rumor going around that I'm an angry young man in a wheelchair. Well, the rumor's true. Now, if you don't want a leg shot out from under you, which I have the right to do because you're trespassing, shake hands and return to your homes."

Billy Ray and Edmund watched each other warily, then the Golden Gloves boxer stuck out his hand and the brawler finally shook it.

"In case your wives ask, both of you won."

Problem was that when Billy Ray arrived home, Grace didn't believe him, but she did smile while taking a steak from the icebox. Things, however, didn't work out as well for Edmund once he discovered his wife hadn't sent any telegram.

Fuming, Edmund went next door to await the return of James Stuart. After a few drinks from the bar, he fell asleep in the study.

The next thing he knew, James was sticking the barrel of one of his revolvers in his face. The Webley Mk VI had proved to be a hardy and reliable weapon in the muddy trenches of the Great War, and James had brought a couple of them home.

"You wanted to see me?"

* * *

"Coming to the swearing in?" Byrnes had won the runoff by three thousand votes, but it was some time before Coley Blease had conceded. He believed votes had been thrown out in Charleston County.

"I could use your support, James, especially those two Webleys you always carry. With the number of protestors prowling the city, the Capitol police have been issued shotguns and tear gas. Washington is an armed camp."

"And Hartleigh was looking forward to the trip."

"Bring her to Roosevelt's inauguration."

James laughed. "You sound pretty certain about that. I heard Bernie Baruch is supporting Newton Baker, Woodrow Wilson's former secretary of war."

"Still some work to do there." The senator-elect became more serious. "I've never seen the country in such a state. Everywhere Maude and I travel we see more and more homeless people, many of them carrying firearms."

* * *

On a shopping excursion along King Street, Christian and Rachel ran into Royce Craven and Eileen Stuart. The couples howdied, made the appropriate sympathetic sounds about Lee Randolph, and how sad it was that so many shops had closed. Once again, as in the long-ago past, the latest fashions were viewed in catalogues, ordered from Paris, and arrived in boxes from overseas.

Rachel knew the perfect dress for Eileen's trousseau, so the two men were left smoking cigars on the street corner. After a meaningless conversation about the theory of technocracy and how quickly a bunch of technocrats could turn around the economy, the two men finally got around to discussing the Craven plantations.

Royce pointed out the differences between rice, upland cotton, and tobacco, and Christian listened to each and every suggestion. Since folks had heard that Christian planned to return to the land, more than one had advice to give, and Christian always listened.

"Not that I disagree with your decision," said Royce, "but why didn't you choose the Belle ancestral home over my two plantations?"

"The overseer at Cooper Hill spent two years at Clemson Agricultural College. I don't feel right about taking his job, especially in this economy. Besides, he's opened up the Belle family library to me."

Royce nodded. "I've heard that the Belles kept extensive journals about their agricultural experiments."

"I've also spent a few afternoons over at Drainland."

"Ah, yes," said Royce, letting out a breath of blue smoke, "the agricultural station between Summerville and Jedburg."

"The overseer at Cooper Hill says this is no time to specialize as they did in the past: rice, cotton, and finally tobacco. He's converting the marginal lands to soybeans, corn, wheat, peanuts, and hay so that Cooper Hill will, once again, be self-sufficient as it had once been under Jennie Belle."

"Jennie Belle?" In his head, Royce counted back generations, trying to remember names. "Don't know the woman. I always thought it was the Franklin Belle of that generation." He clapped the younger man on the shoulder. "Well, because you're a Yankee, I hope you'll be able to break with any of our hidebound traditions."

Rachel and Eileen returned in time to hear the subject of the men's conversation.

Polite comments were made, but Rachel only shook her head wearily. "Evidently, if you're a Yankee, you must have the appearance of being independent."

Once the two couples parted, and after studying the remaining clothing in the window of yet another dress shop going out of business, Rachel said, "You know, darling, you haven't made any suggestions as to what you want in our new home."

"Because you put down your foot rather firmly about installing a swimming pool."

"An extravagance, my dear."

"But you would've owned the first swimming pool in Charleston, and that's the heart of the Belle tradition, isn't it, being the firstest with the mostest?"

Rachel leaned off Christian's arm and regarded him. Her husband was learning how to play the game. Hugging his arm and continuing down the sidewalk, Rachel saw Tessa Stuart and Dory Campbell approaching them. When they stopped to speak, Rachel quizzed the girls as to the whereabouts of their escort. Dory's eyes hardened, but Tessa merely smiled.

"Uncle James said we're free to shop King Street but not to venture anywhere near Market Street."

"I would think not," commented Rachel.

Christian chuckled, and all three women looked at him. He said, "Rachel has closed many a speak on that street."

"Christian, these girls have little interest in ancient history."

"Can you do the Charleston?" asked Tessa, eyes sparkling.

Dory chimed in. "And the Black Bottom?"

"And that new one," added her husband, nodding,

"the Lindy Hop. You need stamina if you marry Rachel Belle."

"Christian, that's quite enough!"

"Oops!" said Christian. "Overstepped my bounds."

"I would say so!"

Dory turned away, but Tessa curtsied. "With your permission." And she quickly followed Dory down the street where they ducked into a malt shop.

Watching them go, Christian said, "That was not one of your more stellar moments, my dear."

"You know that I don't care to be portrayed as common."

Rachel took his arm. "But let's not stand here as if we have nothing to do or nowhere to be." Again they started down the sidewalk with Rachel smiling and nodding to just about everyone.

Her husband asked, "Are you aware of how cross you've become since we moved in with the Stuarts?"

With a smile on her lips and a nod to an approaching couple, Rachel said, "As you know, I have many social obligations."

Again Christian laughed. "As your husband I also know."

She glanced at him. "Do you object?"

"Yes, but not for the reason you think."

"And what do I think?"

"You're unhappy over what you cannot get done."

"I'm just feeling a bit stressed."

"Oh, spare me the Sigmund Freud."

Rachel pulled him to a stop. "Christian, why are you being so disagreeable?"

"Have you ever considered the fact that an unhappy marriage is a lifetime sentence?"

Rachel stared at him for the longest, then said, "Hail a cab."

"Are you feeling unwell?"

"Just hail the damn cab!"

Christian did and ordered the cabbie to return them to the Stuart home on South Battery.

"No, no!" said his wife. "Have him take us to the house on High Battery."

"The one that's being remodeled?"

"Yes," said Rachel, "I may wish to throw a few things."

THIRTEEN

Once Jim Byrnes had been sworn in, many of the senior senators crossed the floor of the Senate to welcome his return to Washington; later in the day, a dinner would be held in his honor.

Peering over the railing as he and Maude Byrnes sat in the Senate gallery, James asked, "What the devil's going on down there? It's like old home week."

Maude flashed a flinty smile. "If you think that's something, just wait until my husband's appointed to the Appropriations Committee and the Banking and Currency Committee. I know you've come to politics late, but Jim's been laboring in the Democratic vineyards since before he was old enough to vote. 'Pitchfork' Ben Tillman gave Jim his start, but Bernard Baruch made it possible for him to move beyond the parochial."

Maude was right about one thing. James did not understand landlubber politics and he'd have to apply himself in Washington, as if learning a new language.

"We'd hoped you'd stay on, James. You were invaluable in turning out the vote in the low country."

"Oh, I don't know. That broadcast on election eve by Jim on Charlotte's WBT reached one hell of a lot of voters—sorry for my French, but that speech was the final nail in Coley Blease's coffin. Coley complained of outside money pouring into Jim's campaign, of votes being thrown out in Charleston, but what it actually came down to was radio."

Maude took the young man's arm and squeezed it. "The votes *allegedly* thrown out in Charleston."

When James joined Byrnes for a nightcap at his home, they retired to the study to smoke a couple of Cubans and drink a glass of bourbon.

"Three generations ago," said Byrnes, "our state was left in ruins by the Union Army. Now, I don't care what opinion you have of the war, I just want to know if you'll help me funnel a larger than usual portion of the federal treasury to South Carolina. When the Democrats throw out the Republicans, we'll control the purse strings, and the first thing Roosevelt will set about doing is sharing that largess—"

"With the poor and the disadvantaged," cut in James. "Yes. I've heard him speak."

"No," said Byrnes, shaking his head. "Once the Democrats control the government, Roosevelt will begin to tax the rich—"

"But won't that hurt the recovery?"

"Franklin Roosevelt blames the business community for all the ills in this country. He'll tax the businessman to death, even after death, and then he'll take that money and give it to those who'll reelect him. A lot of that money will go to create new jobs in the cities of the East and out West. It's the West and urban areas that are up for grabs. The South will never again vote Republican."

"That's the most cynical explanation of politics I've ever heard."

Byrnes took a long draw off his Cuban. After letting out a breath, he said, "You're a valuable asset, James, and I'd hate to lose you, but you must learn that the government goes where the money is and spends where the votes are."

"But why isn't Hoover doing that? He accomplished great things before we put him in the White House, especially the Belgian food relief and again with the flood in the Mississippi River Valley, but all we hear from the White House these days is gloom and doom, not hope and recovery."

"The current generation of Republicans doesn't know how to deal with anything but prosperity. That's all they've known for the last ten years."

"But Hoover sounds angry when he's on the radio."

"Well, are you happy with the way things are?"

"Of course not, but I'm not angry."

"Aren't you, James? After the Panic of Twenty-nine our lives will never be the same."

James considered this. Was it possible that bootlegging had insulated him from the life of the ordinary Joe? After all, it was Byrnes who had to point out the destitution all around him.

"Now, James, before you leave, ask Lewis Belle to come aboard"—Byrnes smiled—"if he's willing to spend a considerable amount of time in the state of Mississippi. Lewis will have to pay his own way and be away from his family for long periods of time, but on the plus side he'll become overly familiar with a multitude of train timetables."

James knew a challenge when he heard one. Picking up his cigar, he took a long drag and blew the smoke in Jim Byrnes's direction. "I'll see your railroads and raise you one company plane. Stuart and Company owns a Ford Tri-motor."

Byrnes studied the younger man.

"My family's lived in Charleston eleven generations, Jim, and it's only the second time, the first being the period of reconstruction, that the head of the house has considered moving to more profitable shores. But with a worldwide recession, there's nowhere to go, and believe me, I've looked."

Byrnes finally smiled. "Do you have a pilot for that plane?"

"Katie Stuart. She reports for the *Piedmont* in Greenville."

"I know Katie. She wrote several nice pieces about me." Byrnes settled into his chair again. "What's her family situation?"

"Three sons. One attends the Citadel, another attends Carlisle Military School in Bamberg. The third's in a private school in Greenville."

"Do I dare upset their family applecart? Would her husband allow her to come aboard?"

"If she wants to. He's totally devoted to her. You've heard of the Old Maids' Club?"

"In Greenville, right?"

James nodded. "The last of the three sisters runs their boarding house with the help of Katie's youngest. She'll keep an eye on him."

After another drag on his cigar, Byrnes said, "I hear Maude had a come-to-Jesus talk with you. You sure politics suits you?"

"I'm an engineer by training so I love projects."

"Well, there's no more important project than holding the South for Roosevelt in Chicago. He must win on the first few ballots or he won't win at all."

"I don't think I understand."

"The Democrat nominee must garner 60 percent of the ballots, but favorite sons from a variety of states can drain away votes from that 60 percent. So the idea is to win on the first two or three ballots or you end up with a deadlocked convention. Then the decision moves into smoke-filled rooms where the bosses compromise, usually on a nominee who doesn't have a chance to win the general election. It happened in 1920 and '24."

"You Democrats need to eliminate the 60 percent rule."

Byrnes shook his head. "The South engineered that rule so they'd hold the balance of power in any nomination. Southerners may not be able to run for president, but we approve the nominee. The fly in the ointment is Speaker of the House John Nance Garner of Texas. William Gibbs McAdoo, Woodrow Wilson's son-in-law, is holding the California delegation for Garner. So it's going to be tight. I'll need you and Lewis in Chicago. The South Carolina delegation will take the 'Carolina Special,' and you and Hartleigh are welcome to come along."

"I have a sixteen-year-old niece who wants to join us. She worked on the campaign."

"That's just about the age when I got involved in politics."

"I don't want to mislead you, Jim. There's a boy attending the University of Chicago . . . ."

Byrnes laughed. "Isn't there always? Well, at least you have Hartleigh to keep an eye on her."

James leaned forward, forearms on knees. "But Bernard Baruch supports former Secretary of War Newton Baker."

"Actually, Bernie's hedging his bets. He's supporting both Newton Baker *and* Albert Ritchie in an effort to stop Roosevelt. Bernie doesn't believe Roosevelt has the experience to be president. He talks about Roosevelt like he's some kind of community organizer instead of the governor of the most populous state in the Union.

"On our side, we have Huey Long of Louisiana, along with James Farley, who knows every Democratic delegate in all forty-eight states. Senator Joe Robinson, the favorite son of Arkansas, might be persuaded to support Roosevelt. That would be your and Katie's assignment. Stay with Arkansas right through the count."

"Okay, but Governor Ritchie held a big rally in Columbia. Don't we need to counter that support?" Albert Ritchie had become famous for his public support for the repeal of Prohibition.

Byrnes shook his head. "That was Bernie's doing. He called in some markers." Byrnes chuckled. "I had to travel all the way to Albany to calm down Roosevelt and Jim Farley. They, too, wanted a rally held for Roosevelt, but I told them you never tell the people of South Carolina who to vote for. You preen around in front of them and hope they like what they see."

"You went to Albany? There wasn't anything about it in the newspapers."

"Of course not. Al Smith's people would've crucified me for giving aid and counsel to the enemy."

James sat there for the longest, trying to process all this information. "But Bernie gave you the money to buy all that radio time to defeat Coley Blease."

Byrnes smiled. "Kind of ironic, isn't it? Bernie put me in the Senate, but I'll be going toe to toe with him in Chicago."

FOURTEEN

A t the corner of East Bay and Columbus, a crowd
waited for the delegation that had made the
journey to Washington for the swearing in of Jimmy
Byrnes. South Carolina had finally sent a senator
to Washington who understood the levers of power
and would operate them in favor of South Carolina.
The reception group included the mayor, the mayor
pro tem, Burnet Maybank, and the rest of the city
council. There was even a brass band.

James was looking for Alexander and a way to
avoid the crush on the platform when he saw his wife
searching the faces of the disembarking passengers.
As far as James was concerned, hers was the only
face that stood out, and he felt a pang of remorse.
Perhaps he should've called home more often while
in Washington, but long distance telephone calls
were extremely expensive.

James let the flow of the crowd carry him off the train and in Hartleigh's direction. Over the welcoming shouts and the blaring of horns, you could barely hear the brass band. A breeze off the harbor caused James to turn up the collar of his topcoat.

Hartleigh saw him, pushed her way through the crowd, and threw herself into his arms. That was followed by a big hug and a passionate kiss—right in public.

"Oh, darling, I've missed . . . ." Her voice trailed off as she glanced at his chest, backed away, and touched her bosom. "James, are those your Webleys?" Hartleigh had learned a long time ago that her husband did not care for the word "guns," preferring "weapons" or their proper names.

James had his fedora and briefcase in one hand and his free hand around her waist. "Sorry. Forgot I was still wearing them."

Hartleigh gave him a wicked smile. "You have nothing to fear from me. I'll gladly submit to you, my lord and master."

Oh, my, thought James, then let's head for home.

"Mister James," said Gabriel, "your chit."

James fished a piece of paper from his pocket and gave it to the footman. As he did, Dory Campbell and Tessa Stuart herded family and friends into an ad hoc receiving line. Other people on the platform stared at those forming the impromptu line. The brass band played even louder.

Hartleigh spoke into James's ear. "Don't be angry, darling, but the day after you left, we had a small memorial service for Lee at St. Michael's, and there were a good number of tears. Thankfully, it stopped Tessa's sobbing. I really thought she'd never stop crying."

At the head of the receiving line stood his mother, who had one glove off and flashed a new diamond ring.

James kissed her cheek and shook Royce Craven's hand. "Did you set a date?" he asked his mother.

Eileen beamed. "No lady accepts a ring without a date."

Royce nodded. "During next spring's festival of flowers."

Next to them stood his sister and her husband, Edmund. Sue Ellen gave her brother a hug, but his brother-in-law chastised him.

"That was a dirty trick you played on me about my mother being ill."

"James," said his sister, "I want you to convince Edmund that he should join Stuart and Company and leave that wretched desert behind him."

"There will be an opening," called Christian from farther down the line.

"Not Cooper Hill?" asked James, moving toward him.

Rachel shook her head. "No. My husband's too pigheaded." Rachel radiated the Belle beauty with her raven hair, porcelain skin, and rich blue eyes. "We've moved into the house on High Battery. I hope you won't miss us."

"Which frees up a room for me," said Tessa, stepping forward to give him a hug. "What should I call you? Daddy?"

"You only have one daddy. I'm your uncle."

Dory cleared her throat. "You know, Captain Stuart, I could use an uncle, too."

Moving along, Elizabeth Randolph smiled at James. "I hope you'll be in Charleston long enough to advise me on my investments. I've done so poorly in the past."

"Of course," said James. Now that was a bit too much. What the devil was going on here?

Polly and Prescott Mitchell agreed to remain in Charleston until the newlyweds returned from their honeymoon.

"Royce says they're going on a round-the-world trip," said Polly, "so we'll be here until they return."

James was visibly relieved. "Thank you, Polly."

Last were Alexander, Pearl, and their children: Benjamin and Chloe. All shook James's hand, but it was Chloe who grabbed his leg and hugged it.

"The twins?" asked James crossing the platform to the car.

"Too windy and too late," said their mother. "You'll see them soon enough in the morning."

And they were off for home, where later that night Hartleigh welcomed her husband into their bed, and once they'd finished celebrating, they cuddled.

"I'll be damned if the place isn't running more smoothly than when I left."

Hartleigh glanced at the bassinettes and put a finger to his lips. "Please don't use such language. We have children now."

"Well, it's true."

Hartleigh slid out of his arms. "None of what you did for Lee Randolph before you left Charleston was necessary, except, perhaps, dispatching Lee's body with haste to the coroner. I understand you felt you must take charge, but there's a limit to how much a man can do." She leaned on her palm supported by her elbow. "You know, I'm more than just a pretty face."

"As I'm learning." Mirroring her position with a palm and elbow, he asked, "What's this about Dory becoming my ward?"

"You're the one who opened that can of worms. Only you can make it go away, but I will warn you that you run the risk of disappointing a teenager."

"Tessa's my niece. She has nowhere to go."

"Oh, please, James, Tessa could've continued living next door. Remember what Polly said."

"Don't take offense, my dear, but having Rachel and Christian living here, along with your mother and Dory Campbell, that's not my idea of family life."

"But Rachel and Christian had no place to go."

"Only to the Belle mansion down the street."

"And my mother to the Charleston Hotel?" Hartleigh scooted against the headboard, propping up on her pillow, and her husband mirrored her again. "You know Mother lost everything in the market. Is that what you want for her?"

James said nothing. If his wife didn't understand, then he would rather smoke a cheroot and catch up on past issues of the *Charleston Post & Courier*. "I apologize for the way I handled the death of Lee Randolph, but I knew his type."

"You don't think I didn't. I don't want to speak ill of the dead, but I know a rake when I see one. You must learn to trust me. Marriages are built on trust."

"Hartleigh, how can you believe I don't trust you?"

"You don't act like it."

James didn't know what to say. How had this conversation gone south so quickly? "Are you saying you want me to prove that I trust you?" Then why had the fool girl married him?

Hartleigh looked at the bassinettes with their twins. Those darlings were under her protection and she under James's. Why didn't he understand? She'd do anything for her babies.

Her husband said, "I couldn't say anything before I left because you were hysterical. You can't tell anyone anything when they're hysterical."

She turned on him. "But you must understand—"

"Were you hysterical or not? Just answer the question."

Hartleigh came off the headboard, sat up, and crossed her arms and hugged a pillow. "You don't have to be so mean about it."

Her husband didn't relent and repeated his question.

"All right, all right," said Hartleigh, shaking her head, "I admit I was a little upset."

"And your mother can worm anything out of you."

"James, don't bring my mother—"

"I set a Pinkerton on Randolph."

That stopped her.

"And the Pinkerton discovered Lee was bosom buddies with Billy Ray Craven. They went out drinking and gambling together." James raised a finger when Hartleigh opened her mouth. "Billy Ray, however, would not join him in any brothel."

"Of course not. Billy Ray's a married man."

Oh, my, thought James. Beyond initiation into the carnal side of life, brothels were rarely patronized by attractive bachelors. They had their hands full with all those girls who wanted to be talked into having carnal relations. "The Pinkerton reported one occasion when Billy Ray's wife, Sue Ellen, joined them in a speak."

"Well, that's not . . ." Both hands came up. "Sue Ellen? You don't say."

Her husband said nothing. A stack of newspapers lay on the nightstand, but he'd never have a chance to read them.

"Oh, I simply can't believe it!" Hartleigh was truly alarmed.

"So I sent a telegraph to Edmund, insinuating that his mother was at death's door and signed Sue Ellen's name."

"You didn't. Oh, James, that was so terribly wrong."

"I'm responsible for my sister."

"But—"

"But nothing!" He sat up. "I'd lie, cheat, and steal and do anything else to protect my family!"

Startled, Hartleigh leaned away from him.

"And that damn Lee Randolph tried to . . . ." That was as far as he got. He slammed his fist into the mattress.

"Lee tried to do what?" Again Hartleigh's hand was at her mouth. She visibly trembled.

"Lee started out by holding hands, then stealing a kiss or two, and then he tried to force himself on Tessa."

"Oh, my." Hartleigh shrank back.

"And when Tessa resisted, Lee was not pleased."

"So you wanted Lee out of Charleston?"

"No. I wanted him dead!"

"Oh, James, take it back!" Her head shook violently, left and right. "Even thinking something like that is a mortal sin."

James whirled around on her. "He touched my niece improperly!"

Hartleigh's hands went to her ears. "No, no, no! I don't want to hear . . ." Her hands came down. "Wait a minute, is that what Tessa told you?"

"You really think a girl's going to admit that to a grown man? She probably wouldn't even tell you. Or Sue Ellen."

"But she needs to trust . . . ."

He flashed a sardonic smile. "Someone who tells her mother everything?"

"James, I'd never . . . ." This was a James Stuart she'd never seen before. She must calm him down before this got out of hand.

"Men trying to take advantage of her," muttered James, his back to her. "Well, not any longer. They'll soon learn Tessa's under my protection."

Hartleigh had never seen her husband in such a state. His shoulders had tensed up causing her to draw back. Not only did James frighten her, but it brought back all her mother's disdain for the Stuarts.

"The Stuarts are rough trade," her mother had

said. "Stuart women are of low morals and the Stuart men are worse. They're wife beaters, drunkards, and liars." And finally, "Nothing good can ever come of a woman who marries into the House of Stuart."

Left unsaid was the fact that Elizabeth had been infatuated with James's father, but her attentions had never been reciprocated. Later, as a young bride, Elizabeth had come to live in the house next door and had had a front-row seat to the degradation of James's mother, Eileen.

James left their bed, snatched up his clothing, and headed for the door. "I'll sleep on the boat tonight."

Hartleigh didn't protest. And she couldn't stop trembling, that is, until she crawled in bed with her mother.

Waking up, Elizabeth asked, "And where are the children?"

Hartleigh sat bolt upright. Hurrying out of her mother's bed, she returned to her bedroom, snatched down her robe from its hanger, then pushed one bassinette and pulled the other into her mother's bedroom.

The next thing Hartleigh knew the sound of shrieking came from the hallway. Her mother leaped from the bed as the twins began to cry.

"Take care of the babies," ordered her mother, slipping into her dressing gown.

Hartleigh glanced at the bassinettes, then the door. The shrieking continued even as her mother left the bedroom.

In the hallway Elizabeth found Tessa standing in the open doorway of Hartleigh's bedroom with Dory trying to comfort her.

Elizabeth took Tessa's arm and tried to reason with her, but soon realized Tessa was sleepwalking.

She slapped her.

Dory stepped back, actually took several steps back. She, too, had been on the receiving end of one of those blows.

Tessa stopped shrieking, but she could not stop snuffling. From the bedroom came the cries of the twins.

Elizabeth handed a linen handkerchief to Tessa. "Dory, go help Hartleigh get the twins back down."

Dory did.

"And close that door." Again Elizabeth took Tessa's arms and faced her. "What is it, child? Did you have a bad dream?" Elizabeth hadn't seen Tessa in such a state since they'd seen Lee Randolph's body off for Richmond. Only when they'd returned to the house had the teenager stopped trembling.

Nodding, Tessa asked, "Where's . . . where's Uncle James?"

Elizabeth glanced through the open door. "I believe he slept on his yacht last night."

Elizabeth had no idea if this was true or not, but finished with her daughter, her son-in-law had probably gone gallivanting down Market Street.

Still, Elizabeth wasn't prepared for Tessa to break away, cross the hall, and head downstairs.

"Tessa, come back here!"

Elizabeth followed the girl to the head of the stairs. With the Andersens gone and Lee Randolph dead, there was no one upstairs but she and the overnight maid.

"Tessa!"

At the railing she saw Tessa disappear toward the rear of the house. To the overnight maid, she said, "Follow her."

The girl did, rushing downstairs.

There was a scurrying below them, and Elizabeth only had time to yell for Tessa to stop before the teenager ran out the front door. The girl had evidently checked the study, and finding no one there, was headed for the marina. The overnight butler wandered into her field of vision, looking perplexed.

"Have a footman and a houseboy go after her," ordered Elizabeth. "One of them is to report back to me as to Tessa's whereabouts."

"Yes, ma'am."

The following morning, Elizabeth paid a call on the Stuart yacht where she found Tessa sleeping in James's bed and James in the bathroom shaving.

Her son-in-law wiped off shaving cream as he stepped into the lounge. "I don't mind if the girl sleeps here." James meant that. At least one person in his household still had some use for him.

Elizabeth turned her back on him. "Please make yourself decent."

James reached into his cabin, took down a shirt, and shrugged into it. Only then did Elizabeth face him again.

She said, "I could forbid the girl from sleeping here, but I don't think that's going to work, not if she continues to have nightmares, and if she should remain on this boat, it'll appear to our neighbors that I cannot run an effective household."

"Well, what shall we do?" James was stone-faced, offering no encouragement.

"Return to your wife's bed as your husbandly duties require."

James smiled. "And the performance of my duties?"

"My daughter's not to be forced to do anything she does not care to do."

"And my needs?"

Elizabeth's face colored and she turned on her heel and headed for the companionway. "I'm quite

sure you're acquainted with every brothel in the city."
Before she went up the ladder, she added, "Please
wake Tessa. I'll await her upstairs."

"Topside."

"Yes, yes, of course."

Once the girl arrived topside, Elizabeth took
Tessa home, quite satisfied with the conclusion of
this incident.

But that was not the end of it. The following week
Alexander picked up the two teenagers from Ashley
Hall and delivered them to the Charleston County
Courthouse, one of the four corners of the law at the
intersection of Meeting and Broad streets.

Outside the courthouse waited a grizzled sea captain, who Tessa immediately recognized. She rushed
into his arms. Jeb Stuart swept up his daughter and
whirled her around.

Setting her down, Jeb said, "What a lucky girl!
You are to have two fathers."

"I . . . I didn't know if you'd come or not."

"Have I ever missed one of your special days?"

Tessa had to admit that, though her father was
often at sea, he had never missed a birthday, a
Thanksgiving, or a Christmas. After another hug,
they went into the courthouse.

Dory had a similar reunion with her younger
brother, who reported that he now worked in the
Stuart and Company warehouse.

"But where do you sleep?" asked Dory.

"They have bunk beds. I've got the upper," he
added proudly.

Dory looked him over. "Is that how you paid for
your Sunday-go-to-meeting suit?"

"Right!" Her brother placed his hands on his
hips, turning this way and that way. "I look like a
real dandy, don't I?"

"Absolutely!" Remembering their older brother had joined the navy, the plight of their remaining sibling hit home. "But what will Bill do?" asked Dory. "He's the only one helping Daddy."

Her brother took her arm and they followed Tessa and her father into the courthouse. "You can't save everyone, kiddo."

Inside a courtroom the Stuart family waited: Eileen and her fiancé, Royce Craven, Sue Ellen and her husband, Edmund.

Elizabeth expected this but not the appearance of several Belles of Charleston. Just when she thought she could categorize the Stuarts, she learned they had another trick up their sleeve.

Because they were joined by the marriage of her daughter and Eileen's son, Elizabeth sat beside Eileen who leaned over to ask, "Is Tessa sleeping through the night?"

"Of course. I wouldn't have it any other way."

Eileen patted Elizabeth's knee. She smiled. "You always were a good neighbor."

Tessa came in the courtroom and took a seat at a table beside her father. Dory arrived on the arm of her brother and they took seats flanking a gaunt, middle-aged man who rarely spoke during the proceedings and never once smiled. Across the room at another table sat James Stuart and Billy Ray Craven, the assistance county solicitor.

Elizabeth asked, "Is all of this really necessary?"

"Some might think not, but this is a day when these girls' lives change." Eileen gestured at the tables on the other side of the railing. "This is Sue Ellen's doing—the physical moving from one family to another is symbolized by moving from one table to another.

"Remember all those plays our children put on?

My Sue Ellen and your Mary Anne fought over who was to play the lead."

The judge entered the chamber and the bailiff said, "All rise."

They did, and it didn't take long for Dory and Tessa to leave their fathers' tables and move across the room to sit in chairs flanking James Stuart.

FIFTEEN

1932

In Portland, Oregon, a former army sergeant, Walter W. Waters, could not find work. He couldn't find work in the canning business; he couldn't find work anywhere. And his bank had closed its doors. But Walter had an ace in the hole. He'd served in the American Expeditionary Force in Europe and had an honorable discharge with the promise of a bonus to be paid in 1945. Lately, Walter had been talking up the idea that Congress should pass a law enabling those "bonuses," actually life insurance policies, to be immediately paid to all veterans. But having served in the army, Walter knew it would be a long, hard slog. The government must be motivated.

President Hoover had excelled at relief overseas as chairman of the Belgian Relief Effort. It seemed to Walter that all he had to do was gather a bunch of veterans from the Great War, travel to Washington, and present their case to the president. Walter talked up the idea on the radio and his message spread like wildfire, especially to South Carolina, a state that always sent a disproportionate share of its young men off to any war.

Hundreds of South Carolinians hopped freight cars to the nation's capital and, if not thrown off by the bulls, answered the clarion call of Walter Waters. There were over 17,000 veterans in Washington and 26,000 camp followers or associated groups who supported the immediate payment of the bonus to the veterans.

The chief of police, himself a veteran of the Great War, sympathized with the marchers and provided tents and food to those camping on Anacostia Flats, a swampy, muddy area on the other side of the Anacostia River, and thousands of veterans remained in Washington even after the Senate tabled a bill passed by the House to grant the bonuses, killing the bill for that session. When the Bonus Army heard these results, many of them drifted home, but some refused to leave either the Flats or the empty government buildings lining Pennsylvania Avenue.

President Hoover ordered the buildings cleared, a riot broke out, and two veterans were killed. And since the police could not thoroughly clear the buildings, the army was brought in, and the army's usual paranoia was inflamed by rumors that anarchists planned to blow up the White House.

General Douglas MacArthur, commanding a thousand soldiers, including staff aide, Dwight David Eisenhower, and six tanks commanded by George S. Patton, rolled down the street during the evening rush hour, and using sabers, bayonets, and tear gas, forced the veterans out of the government buildings. Commuters leaving work for the day shouted: "Shame, shame! Shame on you!"

At the Anacostia Bridge, MacArthur was ordered (twice) by Hoover not to cross the bridge. The army stopped. Not because of orders from the White House, but to give the women and children a chance to disperse. Then the tear gas flew and the army and its tanks rolled across the bridge and into the Flats to clear the area, burning the very tents loaned to the veterans by the city. To get away from the soldiers and their tanks, the veterans and their camp followers ran down Good Hope Road for the safety of Maryland.

Later, at the War Department, MacArthur held a press conference with a definite self-congratulatory air. The press, not amused, accused the army of heavy-handedness, and that weekend at military get-togethers the press was roundly condemned for failing to grasp the fact that the army had just saved the country from a communist takeover. This made even more sense to the military when signs painted on public buildings began to appear: Vote Communist!

When Roosevelt heard of the army's push across the Flats, he confided in an aide: "MacArthur has just prevented Hoover's reelection."

Later in the day, when Huey Long called to berate FDR for appealing to the party's right wing, Roosevelt had to placate the Kingfish, who never missed an opportunity to promote his "share the wealth" scheme, a concept that would redistribute income.

Off the phone, Roosevelt commented that Huey Long was the second most dangerous man in America.

"If Senator Long is the second most dangerous man," asked an aide, "who's the first?"

"Why, the first is General Douglas MacArthur."

Both parties held their national convention in Chicago, and James allowed Dory and Tessa to talk him into leaving for the windy city several days early. Katie flew the Ford Tri-motor into the municipal airport (Midway) where the plane was met by Luke Andersen and Errol Fiske, a blind date for Dory. Fiske, too, was a scholarship student from Wisconsin.

The date was a bust. The car Luke had borrowed overheated and the boys were left behind, waiting for the engine to cool off. A taxi James had rented to follow them into town with the luggage was pressed into service. By the end of the week, however, both couples had fallen madly in love, and the Republicans had slunk out of town with the overwhelming feeling that defeat lurked just around the corner.

The first bit of political intelligence that James gathered from the convention floor was that there was a great deal of interest in a Roosevelt candidacy among the delegates from Illinois, Indiana, and Ohio.

After passing this along to Roosevelt's campaign manager, Farley said, "Fool's gold. The mayor of Chicago, A.J. Cermak, controls all three delegations for Al Smith." Farley clapped James on the shoulder. "Don't be discouraged. Most of what you'll hear will be self-serving drivel, but always bring any information to me."

And snoop James did, learning perhaps more than Jim Farley expected. The night before the opening of the convention, James was headed to Roosevelt headquarters in the Congress Hotel when he passed Sam Rayburn in the hallway. Rayburn was the campaign manager for John Nance Garner of Texas.

James did not pass this along, especially after returning to the Roosevelt headquarters and finding

Farley holding court in the most animated fashion. What was going on with the Texas delegation? Had Farley already struck some kind of a deal?

The following evening, Lewis Belle hovered over the Mississippi delegation while James tailed Senator Huey Long of Louisiana. Katie remained with the Arkansas delegation until Senator Joe Robinson pledged his votes to Roosevelt, then she began following Long. This released James to drift around the convention floor gathering news, rumors, and innuendoes.

The first challenge was to have a pro-Roosevelt delegate appointed to the position of permanent convention chairman. That won, Huey Long, drunk with success or perhaps simply drunk, pressed to abolish the 60 percent rule.

James saw the good sense in this, but the move horrified Roosevelt, Farley, and Byrnes. They quickly disavowed the motion. Now the chance of Roosevelt winning on the first ballot all but evaporated. The Stop Roosevelt crowd, sensing a weakness, would slug it out no matter how many ballots it took.

James returned with scuttlebutt that Bernard Baruch was entertaining Al Smith (former presidential candidate) and William McAdoo (Woodrow Wilson's son-in-law, who controlled the California delegation) with the intent of burying the hatchet between the two men. McAdoo was for John Nance Garner; Al Smith was for, well, himself.

Hearing this, Farley huddled with the Garner people while James returned to the California delegation. Among the Golden State delegates was a young woman who considered James a swell fellow, and through her, James learned that William McAdoo was wavering, and that William Randolph Hearst, the newspaper magnate, did not wish to be left out of any coalition where Roosevelt would be the nominee. Even Joe Kennedy called Hearst and weighed in on the matter.

Tessa and Luke sat in the balcony with Dory, Errol, and Hartleigh and watched Roosevelt fail to garner the necessary 60 percent on the first ballot.

"Oh, Lordy," muttered Tessa, gripping Luke's hand.

On the second ballot, despite the fact that Roosevelt picked up a few votes, the state of Mississippi wavered, and the balance of power in the Mississippi delegation was one vote. If one vote switched in a vote-as-a-unit state, Roosevelt would lose all twenty votes. With cajoling from Lewis Belle, Jim Byrnes, and Strom Thurmond, Mississippi remained in the Roosevelt camp.

Still, Mississippi's governor threatened to bolt on the next ballot, and Katie watched, astonished, as Huey Long promised to come to Mississippi and campaign *against* the governor if Mississippi did not stand fast. (Long later did just that in neighboring Arkansas, and the first woman entered the United States Senate because of his efforts.)

Katie saw the floor managers for Governor Ritchie and former Secretary of War Baker headed in their direction and she alerted Huey Long. Despite what the opposition offered, the Roosevelt faction held fast, though several Mississippi delegates demanded to caucus immediately upon returning to their hotel.

Turned out that the Mississippi delegation could caucus until the cows came home. John Nance Garner, the Speaker of the House, accepted the vice presidential slot, and the following morning, on the fourth ballot, Texas and California swung into the Roosevelt column. Roosevelt had his 60 percent. He'd be the Democratic nominee chosen to unseat a sitting president, Herbert Hoover.

James, exhausted from a lack of sleep, catnapped in Byrnes's hotel room until the phone rang. Actually, it was impossible to sleep because as soon as anyone hung up, the phone rang again with more congratulations. This particular caller was Bernard Baruch.

Byrnes invited the financier over, saying the Roosevelt people would be pleased to see him. So, when the financier's entourage arrived, James hauled himself out of his chair and followed Jimmy Byrnes, Bernard Baruch, and Baruch's chief aide, General Hugh Johnson, over to the Congress Hotel. Within the Roosevelt circle, Byrnes was looked down on as a mere politician who happened to control Baruch's money and must be tolerated.

Going down the hallway, people made way, and General Hugh Johnson, who had become a personal advisor to Baruch after working closely with the financier during the Great War, leaned over to James. "Nice work, Captain Stuart. I always prefer to lose to someone I respect."

Having been around politicians for the last few months, James replied, "Thank you, General, but I've just been holding your place. It's up to people like you to save this country."

Johnson nodded, pushed back his shoulders, and strutted into the Roosevelt suite. The room went silent when the entourage came through the door. Byrnes introduced everyone, and Baruch asked if he could see Roosevelt's acceptance speech. Seeing Baruch contributing suggestions to Louis Howe, Roosevelt's chief political strategist, was enough for James. He stumbled from the suite, rode down in an elevator full of revelers, and took a taxi to his hotel where Hartleigh hustled him off to bed. Before leaving the room, Hartleigh turned on a small fan to muffle the noise of revelers, or so she hoped. Anywhere you went in Chicago, the song of choice for jukeboxes, record players, and anyone who thought they could carry a tune was "Happy Days Are Here Again."

In Miami, Giuseppe Zangara, an unemployed thirty-two year-old Italian bricklayer, walked into a pawnshop and purchased a revolver and a carton of bullets for eight dollars. Showing off the pistol, he told his friends that he hated the rich and the powerful, and if God gave him the opportunity to strike down even one rich man, he'd do it. That opportunity would present itself a few months after the election of a new president.

SIXTEEN

James awoke to find his wife sitting in a chair by his bed. For a moment, he didn't remember where he was.

"Chicago," said Hartleigh. "Franklin Roosevelt was here last night. He accepted the nomination, then flew back to Albany."

James sat up. "Roosevelt was here?" That was nonsense. Candidates never appeared at nominating conventions.

Hartleigh nodded that this was so.

"Where . . . where did you sleep?"

"Right beside you. You were out like a light."

"Well," he said with a smile, "I'm glad to hear that I was a perfect gentleman." James rubbed the sleep from his eyes. "When I'm around such a beautiful woman—"

"James, don't." Hartleigh had not once smiled

since her husband had woken up. She was infuriated that he had not cracked under the pressure of abstinence. Her mother had promised that this would happen—men were, after all, men—and Hartleigh would finally have her husband right where she wanted him.

"Perhaps you could let him catch you in a state of undress," suggested her mother.

"But James spends his evenings in his study and comes to bed late." As silly as it sounded, James had told her that in the army he had learned to sleep fast.

"Well, if he should catch you in the bath, you might ask him to fetch your soap."

"Really, Mother! Must I stoop to cheap theatrics?"

Dory and Tessa came charging into the bedroom and leaped upon the bed. They wore fresh summer dresses from shopping Chicago's Michigan Avenue.

"You missed Roosevelt's acceptance speech," said Tessa, "but Hartleigh took us anyway."

"And Luke?" James turned to Dory. "And that young man whose name I have such a hard time remembering."

"Errol Fiske." Dory feigned disgust.

"Aw, he's just teasing," said Tessa.

Hartleigh stood up from her chair. "You need to give your Uncle James time to prepare for the day. We leave tomorrow."

"Aw, do we have to go?" whined Dory. "I was just getting to know Errol."

Thank you, Dory, thought Tessa with her fingers crossed.

Now it was James's turn to feign disgust. "I've seen the way you girls look at your beaus. You just want to hang around Chicago so you can do more hugging and kissing."

"James!" shouted his wife.

Both girls sat up on the bed. "Oh, no, we'd never!"

"Liars," said James with a grin.

The girls laughed and left the room. After all these years, Tessa was pleased to have a father figure in her life. As for Dory, she didn't completely trust James, but for some reason, she thrived in his care. There would be plenty of time later to test the rules.

"I'll leave you to your toilet." Hartleigh headed for the door.

"No reason to leave." James swung his feet over the side of the bed. "We are man and wife."

Hartleigh frowned as she stormed out of the bedroom. *That man!*

James smiled. With that figure, that face, and the arch of her neck, his wife was more beautiful than ever.

Hartleigh paced back and forth across the sitting room. She simply could not sit still. What infuriated her was how respectful and decent he was toward her. Her mother said it was all a front and he couldn't keep it up. But James had entered her bedroom last night . . . and instantly fallen asleep. Was it possible that she was no longer attractive to her own husband?

She'd thought he'd come to bed to surrender. Now it appeared he never would. Hartleigh returned to the bedroom, entering without knocking.

James only wore boxers. In his hands were his pajamas.

"Sorry." She turned away.

"Come on, Hartleigh, what is it you wish to say?"

Hartleigh let out a breath. "I want to know your intentions."

"You and Katie will return to South Carolina while I'll head on to Washington. With my mother married to Royce Craven and Edmund Hall running the liquor business"—and it went without saying that Sue Ellen was under control—"I have few responsibilities in Charleston."

Hartleigh faced him, faced him and his tanned, rippling muscles that covered a chest with little hair . . . his strong arms and very capable hands. "You don't need to see the twins? They don't need to see their father?"

"Oh," said James, tossing his pajamas on the bed, "I dearly want to see my children again, but I don't wish to interfere with the hatred your mother's instilling in them. It would only confuse them."

Hartleigh didn't know what to do with her hands. She twisted a handkerchief that had somehow found its way into her hands. Her husband stood there for the taking, or taking her.

"James, this can't go on! This is not right!"

James bent over to pick up his shoes, his back rippling with muscles. Hartleigh longed for James to sweep her up in those strong, capable arms and hold her tight. What in the world could she do to get him to hold her again?

No. She would do nothing. She was a Charleston lady who'd given her heart to a rogue.

"And Tessa and Dory?"

"Dory and Tessa will be enrolled in Georgetown. The paperwork has already been approved."

Hartleigh looked away again but could not discern whether she was heating up because of her desire for this man or her anger from realizing that he lacked any physical need for her. After all, he only wore his boxers. "You have no right to do this."

"What I don't have is the right to take the twins away." He smiled. "But I'm working on that."

She faced him. "You wouldn't dare!"

He stepped over, cupped her face with one hand, and put his other hand around her waist. "Hartleigh, if your mother was truly concerned with anyone's well-being, she'd put herself in service to these two motherless girls. But all your mother wants is her life back the way it was before I entered your lives, and that's impossible, so she's set her sights on controlling her world, and that, too, is quite impossible as everyone but your mother learned with the crash of the stock market."

Hartleigh leaned into his hand, strong and powerful. Her eyes closed. There was a world she dreamed of ever since she'd been a small child. Every once in a while she got a glimpse . . . .

When he removed his hand, Hartleigh blinked and almost lost her balance.

"This marriage was doomed from the start. I should've heeded your mother's warning. If your sister had lived, she and I would've eloped, but you, you held back, probably from a sense of propriety, and simply made yourself irresistible. So blame me. I should've been more of a gentleman, but I'm a pirate at heart, and pirates take what they want. That's why we're called pirates."

Returning to Washington, James was immediately summoned to Democratic headquarters on Madison Avenue in New York. Though he arrived after dark, James was ushered into James Farley's office where the political operative signed letters. A small man lay on a sofa smoking cigarettes: Louis McHenry Howe, otherwise known as "the gnome." Farley did not look up. He signed letters six, sometimes eight hours a night. Using his pen, Farley waved James into a visitor's chair.

"Can we commandeer that Ford Tri-motor of yours for the campaign?" asked the campaign manager. Like Ford cars and tractors, the Ford aircraft was well-designed, relatively inexpensive, and reliable.

The Tri-motor could be fitted with skis and floats. It could land practically anywhere.

"Of course."

From the sofa, Howe mumbled something. During the convention, James had often walked in on Farley lying on the floor, head to head with Howe, taking political instructions from the asthmatic man. Electric fans had blown on the two men lying on the floor, and one of the phones had been a private line to Roosevelt in Albany.

Farley's pen never stopped moving. "Same terms?" That meant James paid his own expenses.

"Of course."

"Your pilot's a girl?"

"Katie Stuart. She used to report for the *Piedmont*."

Farley looked up, but his hand continued to scribble and shuffle paperwork. Only occasionally did he glance at the letters in front of him. "I know Bony Peace. He and his sons are dedicated to promoting Greenville as the textile center of the Piedmont."

Howe cleared his throat.

"However, if your pilot's a girl—"

"We'll take along a couple of Katie's sons. They'll love it. Katie can teach them how to fly."

From the couch, Howe grunted his approval.

"Always keep your trips on the up and up, Captain Stuart. By the way," asked Farley, "'Captain' Stuart—is that like a Kentucky colonel, an honorary title?"

"Battlefield promotion; 328th Infantry Regiment, Eighty-Second Division."

Farley stopped writing and stared at him. "You were in the Great War? You don't look old enough."

"Lied about my age. Pershing promoted me when my superiors were killed in a mortar attack. They huddled in a trench, deciding who would hold our position and who would flank the machine gun nest. While they conferred, my squad came under murderous fire. When my buddies on either side of me were killed, I knew the jig was up and charged the nest. I wanted to go down fighting, but I don't remember much of what happened—it was all a red blur—but none of the Krauts were alive when I finished with that particular machine gun nest."

Howe had stopped smoking. Farley's pen had stopped moving. The only sounds came through the door from the secretarial pool.

James shrugged. "Sorry. Freud would say that was my ego talking. I really don't remember much."

Howe grunted something from the couch.

"This didn't get reported in the papers."

James stared into his lap. He was a fish out of water when it came to politics, the naïve new guy, and he'd suffered many a slight or slur from established pols since becoming involved in Roosevelt's campaign, especially having the credentials to move around the floor at Chicago Stadium. The mayor of Chicago had given the Roosevelt people one hundred floor passes; the supporters of Al Smith had received thousands.

James looked up. "The army had Alvin York, who'd captured and killed so many Germans that they just wanted me to go away. I was transferred to observation balloons at the rank of captain. Pershing said the balloonists wouldn't respect anyone below the rank of captain."

Howe's laugh turned into a cough.

Farley chuckled. "From the frying pan into the fire, eh? Get shot down much?"

"Only twice."

Both men stopped laughing. "Then how—"

"We had parachutes, and, unlike the fixed-wing aircraft pilots, we damn well used them. Fixed-wing pilots thought anyone who carried a parachute aloft was a sissy."

The other two men laughed, quite happy to have something to laugh about.

Farley gestured with his pen. "Take these . . . ."

As James reached for the cards, Howe raised a hand with notes scribbled on several sheets of paper.

"Those, too, Captain Stuart."

James took the papers from the man lying on the couch.

"Your job is to work the western states. I'll invite as many party chairmen to New York as will come. While they're here, I'll stress that they're responsible for holding their state for FDR."

"FDR?"

"Franklin Delano Roosevelt. The press came up with that moniker. Guess it saves ink." He returned to signing letters.

James had noticed several fountain pens, cartridges full of ink, lying at the ready, and while James had sat there, a secretary had entered the office and collected a stack of signed letters. According to campaign lore, there were over 140,000 party leaders in the country, and James Farley was determined that each and every one of them would receive a letter personally signed by him.

"Your job, Captain Stuart, is to remind those state chairmen that they alone are responsible for turning out the vote." He looked up from his letters. "Your auxiliary mission is to quash any rumors that the campaign is being run by the DNC, so always introduce yourself as my personal emissary."

"What about Senator Byrnes?"

"This is at Byrnes's suggestion. He recommended you."

Again, Louis Howe grunted from the sofa.

"We'll be listening for any rumors about you and your cousin." Farley returned to his letters. "Don't forget the cards."

James picked up the business cards, nodded to Howe, and left the office. While James waited for the elevator he examined the back of Farley's business cards. All of them read: "This man has my complete confidence" and were signed Jim Farley. Only upon reaching Union Station did it occur to James that the business cards provided an introduction for anyone, and he wondered how many had turned down the job before Byrnes suggested his name. He was, after all, one little cog in an organization with much to do before election day.

While waiting for the train to Washington, James stepped into a telephone booth and placed a call to the Mayflower Hotel.

"Oh, Captain Stuart," said the switchboard operator, "I believe your wife's in the restaurant. Should I switch the call there?"

"Katie Stuart's not my wife. She's my cousin."

"Oh, I'm so sorry. I'll put you right through."

A phone was brought over to Katie's table and plugged in. She, Dory, and Tessa were enjoying a late dinner and speculating about the boys they'd left behind in Chicago. Both girls were completely smitten and couldn't wait for the world's fair to begin. Uncle James had promised them a return trip.

"You do realize," said Katie, "that there's no way those boys would've been able to complete their academic work if you two girls had remained in Chicago."

She picked up the phone. "Yes?"

"You need to get to bed." Katie went to bed early if she flew the following morning. "We just received our marching orders, and they involve the western states, so you'll want to drop by Greenville and pick up a couple of your boys."

"And you?"

"I'll meet you in St. Louis. Florence Belle will make sure the girls attend the last semester of summer school. I don't want them to be at any disadvantage when they start Georgetown in the fall."

Four months later Roosevelt ran the tables on Hoover, and after the election he vacationed on the Astor yacht sailing out of Jacksonville and returning to Miami. When Roosevelt docked, the unemployed bricklayer was waiting for him.

SEVENTEEN

1933

The crowd packed Bayfront Park and cheered their hero. "FDR! FDR! FDR!"

Two Secret Service agents lifted Roosevelt to the rear of the convertible where the crowd could see him much better. Giuseppe Zangara, a little over five feet tall, joined a doctor's wife on a wooden bench. From there, he had a clear shot at the president-elect and the mayor of Chicago. Anton Cermak had come to Miami to beg for money for his schoolteachers who had not been paid in almost a year. Zangara drew the pistol from his pocket and pointed it over the heads of the crowd.

"FDR! FDR! FDR!"

Lillian Cross, the doctor's wife, shifted around, wiggling the bench. This threw off Zangara's aim and his first bullet struck the Chicago mayor instead of the president-elect. Because of this wiggle, Mrs. Cross would later be invited to attend Roosevelt's inauguration.

"He's got a gun!"

Women screamed, men shouted, and the Secret Service shoved Roosevelt off the back of the convertible where the president-elect slid into the backseat. The wounded mayor was pushed away from the vehicle.

By the time Zangara regained his balance, the man standing beside the bench had grabbed his arm. The pistol fired wildly into the crowd. Other spectators went down, one of them a woman who later died from her wounds. Wrestled to the ground, Zangara's arm was pinned down and the pistol taken away.

The Secret Service shouted for the convertible to move out.

"No!" said Roosevelt. "Bring the mayor. He's been hit."

Leaning into the convertible, a Secret Service agent explained that other gunmen might be in the crowd.

"Back up the car!" ordered Roosevelt.

The automobile backed up, the mayor of Chicago was pulled inside, and the convertible sped off. During their trip to the hospital, Roosevelt comforted Cermak.

"Tony, keep quiet—don't move. It won't hurt if you stay quiet." Then later, "Everything's going to be all right."

Everything was not going to be all right. A week later, the mayor died of complications unrelated to the bullet wound, and four months later, Giuseppe Zangara was executed in Florida's electric chair, "Old Sparky."

Zangara's last words were that he did not hate FDR, but that he hated the rich and powerful who must pay for their misdeeds.

Then Zangara shouted, "Pusha da button!"

Katie was glued to the radio in the parlor when James returned from using the phone in the study of the publisher of the *Denver Post*. James had just finished setting up another meeting on their thank-you tour of the western states. On this trip, none of Katie's boys had come along, so Katie and James roomed with families who had more than one guest room and they always traveled with a fellow Democrat.

She looked up from the radio. "The president's been shot."

"Hoover?" asked James.

"Roosevelt."

"Roosevelt's the president-elect."

"Oh, right." Katie slapped her forehead. "How dumb of me."

"What happened?"

"FDR was addressing a crowd in Miami when some guy stepped out of the crowd and emptied his magazine at his limo. Members of the crowd subdued the assassin."

James considered this. "Then pack your bags. We're leaving for Washington."

Katie looked out the window. "We won't get far."

"But we can make Omaha, Nebraska. We'll fly into Washington the following day. Who's our contact in Omaha?"

She reminded him.

"I'll call Omaha, then Greenville to alert the Old Maids' Club." James turned to go. "Anyway, there's nothing we can do with Roosevelt shot. It's all they'll want to talk about."

By the time James finished his phone calls, Katie had their bags packed and taken downstairs. A taxi whisked them to Denver's mile-high airport.

Inside the cab, a relieved driver wiped his forehead. "It wasn't Roosevelt, but the mayor of Chicago who got shot." He glanced into the rearview mirror. "Man, I don't know what this country would do if Roosevelt had been shot. We'd really be in a pickle."

With James out of town, Dory, feeling trapped in the Mayflower Hotel, proposed to Tessa that they sneak out and see more of Washington than its monuments and museums.

"How do we do that?" asked Tessa. "There are hobos on every corner."

"Do as I did in Charleston. Dress like boys. All we need from the thrift store are trousers, caps, shoes, shirts, and to wrap our chests like flappers. We can smear a bit of charcoal on our faces."

"Go in blackface?"

"No, you ninny, we smear charcoal on our cheeks. Boys are nasty. They never wash."

The idea appealed to Tessa's Stuart blood. It was an idea Aunt Sue Ellen would embrace with enthusiasm.

"But where would we change?" asked Tessa. "It's not like there are public restrooms in Washington."

"There's a bellboy who'll let us change at his place."

"Going to a boy's apartment? Are you nuts?"

"Don't worry. He's not like that. He rooms with a guy."

"Which only doubles the odds that we'll be spied on."

"Oh, come on, Tessa. They're sissy boys, and he doesn't want anyone to know, so he won't tell."

As Dory had predicted, the bellboy graciously allowed them to change in his bedroom. Actually, there was only one bedroom, and after looking around, Tessa pushed the boys' living arrangement out of her head. It made no sense to her. Instead, she concentrated on dressing properly, and the bellhop provided a couple of belts the girls had completely forgotten to purchase.

Another hitch Tessa wasn't prepared for: all the sullen men standing around on street corners. The sight so unnerved Tessa that she refused to leave the bus. Since Dory had commandeered the window seat, she simply scooted over, and using her hip, shoved Tessa into the aisle. Actually, Dory wanted to take her friend's hand and lead her off the bus, but boys didn't touch other boys, unless it was to punch another boy in the face.

Leaning into her, Dory said, "This is our stop."

But Tessa held on tight to an overhead strap and stared out the window, noticing that none of the sullen men got on the bus.

From the front, the driver said, "Make up your minds, boys."

Grasping seats on opposite sides of their aisle, Dory thrust her chest into Tessa, forcing her friend toward the rear of the bus and down the steps.

Tessa protested.

"Lower your voice!" ordered Dory.

Reaching the curb, Tessa whispered.

"Not your volume but your tone!"

Tessa glanced up and down the street and saw people staring at them, especially the sullen ones. Did those men suspect that they were girls? And what would they do if they found out?

"Your rubbernecking's drawing attention." That didn't seem to reach her either, so, exasperated, Dory grabbed Tessa's arm and pulled her across the sidewalk and into an alley. Men stared, not lecherously but as though puzzled by their actions.

Behind them, a trashcan tipped over, spewing garbage across the alley. The men on the curb shifted their attention past the girls to where a man and a boy picked through the garbage. Those on the curb began drifting in the girls' direction, then, as they passed, broke into a run and raced down the alley. And if you were to ask these scroungers what they were doing, they'd all give the same answer: It's scraps for my kid's pet rabbit. Still, after the men finished pawing through the garbage, lettuce and spinach leaves were always left behind: the perfect meal for any rabbit.

Dory pulled Tessa from the alley and toward the corner. As they went, Tessa continued to rubberneck and this infuriated Dory even more.

"I swear, Tessa, the farther you are from Charleston the more conventional you become."

But it wasn't the fashionable clothing in the windows that had caught Tessa's eye. There were fewer Negroes in the nation's capital, a lot more panhandlers than she'd ever seen south of Broad, and men selling apples; shoeshine boys were five and six to a block.

My Lord, what would happen if a girl married the wrong man? Who would provide for her? Who would care for her and her babies? And was Luke Andersen such a young man?

"This is what boys experience everyday?" asked Tessa. "They work on—Uncle James calls them projects—among strangers?"

"I guess so. I never thought about it."

"Now," said Tessa, nodding, "I finally understand. Boys seek out us girls so they won't be so lonely."

"Well," said Dory, "there may be a bit more to it than that."

At the corner, Dory pointed down the street. "Look at all those half-naked women. That's got to be the red light district. Let's go take a look."

"Why would I care to see a bunch of half-naked women?"

"Because today you're a boy."

Pushing their way past newsies touting their latest edition, the girls crossed the street. On the other side, people with money ate food served from a window.

"What's this?" asked Tessa. "It's not hotdogs or hamburgers."

"I have no idea."

Tessa sounded out the name on the sign. "New York . . . piz—za."

A businessman took a bite from his slice, awkwardly eating from a sheet of butcher paper and leaning away from his food.

"Hey, boys," shouted the young man from behind the counter. "Slice for a nickel. Best pie in the nation's capital."

The two girls looked at each other. Around them, hungry men shot longing looks at the pies on shelves safely sequestered behind the young man. A cop came along with a short wooden club, encouraging the men to cross to the other side of the street. He ignored both of the girls.

A workman left the counter, grease dripping down the front of his blue work shirt.

"Oh," warned Tessa, "we can't eat that. It's too messy."

Dory pulled her friend over to the counter. "Yes, we can. We're boys and we don't care how we look."

The young man offered a slice of cheese for a nickel, but for a penny more, he'd add pepperoni. "You look like pepperoni guys to me."

The girls smiled and nodded but did not reply. They had no idea what the young man was talking about, but he was kind of cute.

Tessa reached for her purse, realized she had none, and then dug into her pants pocket. Boys' pockets were huge. She gave the young man a dime and Dory added the pennies.

"So," asked the young man, laying out the slices on butcher paper, "you want pop? Bottles are a nickel, but you can return the empties for a penny."

"Er . . . I don't know."

"What you got?" asked Dory.

The young man jerked his thumb at a sign. He served Coke, root beer, and ginger ale. "Take your pick."

Tessa whispered, "I don't think we should drink the beer."

"Two Cokes," said Dory, nodding to the young man.

So the girls stumbled away with both hands full, and almost dropped their slices trying to figure out how to eat from one hand and drink from the other. Where in the world would they sit down?

Evidently Tessa couldn't put the image of the sullen men out of her mind. The following morning Dory found Tessa asleep in James Stuart's bed.

Sitting on the edge of his bed, James was loading the Webleys. He glanced at the teenager. "Tessa had a bad dream." He grinned. "Just what were you girls up to yesterday?"

"Er . . . well," stammered the former runaway, "it might've had something to do with the dinosaur exhibit at the Smithsonian."

And sooner than later the girls' adventures began to filter back to Charleston in letters from Katie Stuart, and because of the ceremony at the county courthouse, Hartleigh Stuart came to realize that her familial responsibilities had somehow shifted from Charleston to Washington, DC.

EIGHTEEN

The front desk clerk smirked when Hartleigh said that she was the wife of James Stuart.

"Really?" He shared his smile with his fellow clerk at the other end of the counter. "Another wife of James Stuart."

Grinning broadly, the second front desk clerk said, "Welcome, Mrs. Stuart!"

Hartleigh didn't know what to make of this. She looked around the lobby as Molly pushed two buggies in her direction and their luggage arrived with the bellhop. "This is the Mayflower Hotel, isn't it?"

James and Katie came through the revolving doors. Katie was laughing at something James had said. Neither of them noticed Hartleigh, the buggies, nor the luggage cart at the desk.

One of the young men raised his voice so it would carry across the lobby. "Captain Stuart, another of your wives has just arrived in Washington!"

James and Katie stopped and stared, and the front desk clerks noted with approval that their smiles turned to frowns.

As they moved toward the counter, James said, "Just when I thought things couldn't get any worse."

"James, please, I'm sure Hoover had nothing to do with this."

James snorted.

"I'll handle this," said Katie.

The front desk manager strolled out of his office, wondering why any employee of the Mayflower Hotel would need to shout across the lobby.

"What's going on out here?"

One of the young men gestured at Hartleigh, who had turned to face James and Katie. "She's Mrs. Stuart, too."

Hartleigh flushed as, once again, she faced the counter.

"Madam, is there something I might help you with?" asked the front desk manager.

"I don't know your customs here at the Mayflower, but these two young men have insinuated that there might be an irregularity in my marriage."

Both clerks protested that they had meant no insult.

James and Katie joined Hartleigh at the counter, and Hartleigh stood on tiptoes and kissed her husband on the cheek, then brushed her cheek against Katie's.

"I insist on an apology." Hartleigh opened her purse. "I have a copy of our marriage license here."

James looked at the clerks, then his wife. "What the hell just happened here?"

"Now, James, watch your language." Hartleigh rummaged around in her purse. "I'm sure it's in here somewhere." Young couples rarely traveled without their marriage license if the trip involved an over-night stay.

The front desk manager glanced at Hartleigh's ring finger. "That won't be necessary. Everyone in the Mayflower knows Captain Stuart." He looked at James who had bellied up to the desk. "I imagine you'll need another key?"

"Two. One for the nanny." James pointed at Molly. "She'll be staying with the twins."

The manager gave the clerks a cold stare until one of them hastily took down keys from the rack behind him. "A rollaway will be sent up."

"Mrs. Stuart," said the clerk, "your husband has a wing of the seventh floor. You'll need this to get off there when no operator is running the elevator."

"Thank you."

Hartleigh reached for the key, but James's hand shot past hers, grabbing the clerk's tie. He jerked down, banging the young man's face into the desk.

The clerk screamed, dropped the keys to the counter, and when his head came up, his nose dripped blood. His boss offered a handkerchief while James took the key off the counter.

To the desk manager, James said, "I've taken care of that one. You take care of the other."

The second clerk backed away, hands rising in his defense. "No, no! I meant no disrespect."

As everyone stared, James tipped his hat to Molly. "Glad you could join us." He reached into the buggies and tickled the twins. "Good to see you, too, kiddos."

The twins reached for their daddy, but he'd taken Hartleigh and Katie's arms and was escorting them over to the elevator with Molly and the buggies trailing behind. The bellhop brought up the rear, and he almost ran over Molly with the cart as he continued to stare at the clerk trying to stanch the flow of blood coming from his nose.

At the counter, the manager said, "Call the house doctor, and once you've done that, you are to report to my office."

"But," protested the uninjured clerk, anticipating how the meeting would go, "he has a whole harem up there."

"Ah, Mrs. Stuart," said the Negro operating the elevator, "did you have a good day?" An older man, he sat on a wooden stool.

"Whether I'm out West or here in Washington, I deal with politicians," said Katie. "So how do you think it went?"

James introduced his wife and Molly.

The black man grinned. "Name's Milo, Mrs. Stuart. I guess you've come to bring a little law and order to the seventh floor."

Hartleigh didn't know what to make of that so she simply smiled as the luggage cart and baby buggies came aboard. As the elevator doors were closing, a woman's arm appeared between the doors, preventing them from closing.

"Whoa!" The operator jammed a button until the door reopened for Susan Moultrie.

"Thank you. Oh, hello, Mrs. Stuart." Glancing at James, she added, "Didn't know you were paying us a visit." Susan Moultrie took her place on the other side of Katie as the crowded elevator rose to the seventh floor.

All of them got off on the seventh floor with Milo offering Hartleigh some final advice. "Remember, Mrs. Stuart, no one can come up here unless they have a key or they're with me. You can use the stairs to walk down or in case of fire, but no one can reach this floor from the stairs because Captain Stuart has had this wing sealed off." He grinned conspiratorially. "Good to know, what with all the young ladies on this floor, right?"

"Er . . . right." Hartleigh had the impression that this Negro wished to be her ally. Or was he simply parroting the hotel's line of defense against the number of young men loitering in the lobby? It'd not been lost on Hartleigh that in every alcove in the lobby, girls were surrounded by young gentlemen. Well, the "gentlemen" part of the equation had yet to be proven.

At the seventh floor their bellhop steered the luggage cart off the elevator, across the hall, and into an open-door suite.

"James took the room across from the elevator," explained Katie. "Make sure your bedroom door is always locked. James sleeps with both the hallway door open *and* his bedroom door open."

Katie took Hartleigh's arm and they started down the hall. "There're three empty suites in this wing. Lewis Belle, his wife, and their girls are in one. The Belles expect Georgiana and Franklin for the inauguration, and the last suite is reserved for whoever's traveling with them. Beyond that is the wall that seals off this wing from the other rooms on this floor."

Katie lowered her voice as they approached the door of Florence and Lewis Belle, Lewis Belle being the Stuart family attorney. "Hotel life does not agree with Florence, but there's no reason why you should feel isolated. Maude Byrnes has a bridge club and Club Eisenhower operates out of the Wyoming Hotel."

"Club Eisenhower?"

"An informal group of military officers, politicians, and government workers who get together once a week. Anyone can attend. And if you have no idea where to go or what to see in Washington, just drop by the Wyoming . . . ." Katie's voice trailed off as she remembered Charleston ladies did not drop by but presented cards. "I'll call Mamie and tell her that I recommended you stop by. There's no more sincere and honest a person than you'll find." Katie grinned. "And the biggest flirt in Washington. All the men love Mamie."

Hartleigh smiled. "I can imagine."

Katie knocked on the Lewis Belles' door and gestured across the hallway. "If your mother should pay a visit, there are at least two suites for her to choose from down here."

"Oh, I can't imagine that she would."

When the door's lock was thrown, Katie quickly added, "Remember how Florence didn't care for the telephone?"

Hartleigh nodded.

"Well, up here she's embraced the instrument with a vengeance. Her long distance charges are astronomical, and I'm someone who knows a thing or two about long distance calls."

A matronly woman opened the door and broke into a smile. "Oh, praise the Lord! Another grown-up." Florence stuck her head out the door and glanced up and down the hallway. "I guess it would be too much to ask for your mother to be with you."

"No mother," said Hartleigh, cheerfully. "Only the babies and me."

The two women air kissed.

"At least I'll have someone to talk to. This one," referring to Katie, "is never home."

"Mrs. Belle, please! I'm a spokesman for Senator Byrnes."

"Women working outside the home." Florence shook her head. "This town is full of them. Well, welcome to Washington, Hartleigh. How old are those twins of yours now?"

"About to turn three."

"I guess Katie's told you that this floor has an unlimited number of babysitters so don't hesitate to call on them. I won't let my girls charge you a dime." She glanced down the hallway. "I'll be down shortly, but first I must conclude a phone call."

Katie's eyes widened, but she did not smile.

Before closing her door, Florence added, "By the way, some of us girls are playing bridge at Maude Byrnes's tomorrow afternoon. If you've recovered sufficiently from your trip, let me know. You'd be a marvelous partner, and there's always a shortage of decent players for two tables."

Once the door had closed, Katie snorted, bent over, and took Hartleigh's arm. The two young women hurried down the hall. "Whenever I visited Charleston with the Old Maids' Club, I spent a lot of time babysitting Florence's girls, and I can guarantee that she can squeeze a dollar until the eagle hollers."

Ahead of them, James tipped the bellboy, and the bellboy and the cart disappeared into the elevator.

"I'm in the last room down on the right if you're up for some girl talk or late night drinking. A lot of late night drinking goes on in this town, and quite a few girls show up in the speak downstairs after dinner."

"You mean streetwalkers?"

Katie shook her head. "That's what I first thought, but it's single girls out looking for a husband. They travel in packs and arrive by taxi."

"How odd."

They passed James standing in the doorway of his suite and removing the rounds from his Webleys. He stuffed the bullets into his pockets and started on the other cylinder, bending down to pick up a round that had gotten away from him. From a room kitty-corner from where his father stood, young James watched this process intently, that is, until

Molly took his arm and pulled him inside. The door closed on his yelp.

"Dory and Tessa are across the hall. Susan Moultrie has a suite of her own across from me, but with the twins arrival, there are no empty suites on this end." She pointed beyond that. "That's the fire exit down the hall, but no one leaves the building without an escort. You might've seen the Bonus Army wandering around town as you came from the train station. I'm sure James will fill you in on the precautions we've taken."

She tugged Hartleigh down the hall and lowered her voice. "James wants to be a knight in shining armor. I know the type. I'm married to one. They can be quite smothering."

This made little or no sense to Hartleigh. Husbands were, by definition, supposed to protect their families.

James shook his head as if he knew what Katie was telling his wife. Everyone thought he was too strict, but those people never took into consideration that the fabric of society had been torn asunder with the stock market crash; everyone had lost their nerve. Young people postponed marriage, but that didn't prevent them from having carnal relations, and another point often overlooked was the fact that the current generation was the first to go on dates in enclosed motor vehicles.

Behind James, the door to his suite remained open, propped back with a cloth-covered brick whose sleeve had been sewn by none other than Susan Moultrie.

"Will the hotel have any trouble with Molly living up here?" asked Hartleigh.

"They have separate restrooms for the colored help on the ground floor and I'm sure a rollaway bed will be sent up. I assume Molly has the proper outfits?"

"Of course. Blue and white striped for mornings and black for afternoons and evenings." Remembering Katie's letters, she asked, "Katie, what's Susan Moultrie doing here?"

"Seeing if she likes Washington." The two young women had reached the far end of the hall and now turned and headed back toward the elevator. "If so, she'll send for her son. Your brother-in-law Edmund fired her. Said she was taking a job from a man. James couldn't bring himself to do it, so his brother-in-law did. I didn't know Susan could type, but she's very good and she takes shorthand. Very admirable for a woman whose family has more than enough money from bootlegging, but Susan wants to make it on her own."

Katie didn't mention that with Hartleigh remaining behind in Charleston, Susan Moultrie was the one who made sure James never dined alone and rounded up enough hands for a weekly game of poker. She also hosted the cocktail hour each evening, and though she was from the wrong side of the tracks—her family had always been merchants—she emulated Katie Stuart to the point of wearing trousers, but only once. Turned out James didn't like women in trousers.

"Senator Byrnes hired her for clerical work," said Katie. "Susan's responsible for adding to the index card file that Maude Byrnes kept while the senator was running for office."

"You work there, too, don't you?"

"Yes." Katie studied Hartleigh. "I'm not going to receive any static from you about working outside the home, am I?"

"If it doesn't bother your husband, what does it matter what anyone else thinks?"

"Oh, believe me," said Katie with another laugh and taking Hartleigh's arm again, "in that regard,

Washington is no different from Charleston, and girls like me learn to stick together." And just as quickly her hand slid from Hartleigh's arm. "I'm sorry. That wasn't intended to sound so mean-spirited."

Hartleigh took Katie's hand as they reached the elevator. "We're family. We'll always stick together, and I'll be happy to meet your friends, that is, if my presence doesn't make your friends uncomfortable."

"That's good. They are a fun lot, and I know I speak for all the women on this floor when I say . . . ."

The elevator doors opened and four girls stumbled out, laughing. They saw Hartleigh and their laughter dried up.

"I was so scared . . . ."

"Me, too."

Were the only words Hartleigh and Katie could make out.

The girls had cut class for the new movie everyone was talking about: *King Kong.* And all of them looked as if they'd been caught with their hands in the cookie jar. Their schoolbooks came up to be clutched across their chests, and the Belle twins and Tessa and Dory stammered their hellos. The four split up, two pairs heading in opposite directions down the hallway. None inquired as to whether the twins had also made the trip.

"Now what do you imagine that was all about?" asked Hartleigh, watching Tessa and Dory unlocking the door to their room.

"I imagine they've been chumming around at the malt shop. They insist on walking to school, and before they arrive on campus, each girl has picked up one or two boys who want to carry her books."

"But that's not proper!"

"Well, before you go off half-cocked, remember they're stuck up here on the seventh floor and very far from home."

"Another reason to control their access to boys."

"Well, think before you act or you'll quickly become the wicked witch from south of Broad. The girls are allowed to take their meals in the restaurant downstairs as long as they eat in twos."

"Really? That and a soda fountain are appropriate venues to meet boys?" Hartleigh realized she'd arrived just in the nick of time.

"Hartleigh, please listen. James, Florence Belle, Susan, and I have checked out that soda fountain. It's the only place the girls can dance to a jukebox and socialize. If you take that away, they'll start cutting classes and lying to us."

"Lying? Ashley Hall graduates would never lie."

NINETEEN

The following day, as the girls prepared to leave for school, Hartleigh, still in her dressing gown, laid down the law.

"All of you are Ashley Hall graduates, and you'll be judged by the standards of Ashley Hall, not Washington, DC. Step out of line and I'll move heaven and earth to return you to Charleston."

The girls were not pleased. They were finished with high school and wanted to get on with their lives—meeting new boys without the constraints of Miss McBee's rules of etiquette.

The twin daughters of Lewis Belle had squandered their opportunities to marry while attending the party of the century, and with few men leaving their cards in Charleston the nation's capital offered a final opportunity for them to land a man under the cover of attending nursing school at Georgetown. Still, the whole process of becoming nurses nauseated the Belle twins, and they were seriously considering becoming schoolteachers.

Hartleigh continued to lecture as Katie left her room at the end of the hall. "I, too, attended Ashley Hall, and we will be guided by Miss McBee's principles in everything we do. There will be no lipstick or fingernail polish. Gloves and hats will be worn at all times. And as for your clothing you so casually drop anywhere in your rooms . . . ."

The elevator doors opened, and Alexander stepped off. "I have the car waiting, Miss Hartleigh."

"We'll finish this conversation once the school day ends. Look for Alexander. He will return you to the hotel."

The Negro held open the elevator doors and the girls stepped aboard and descended to the lobby, none of them looking pleased.

After the doors closed, one of the Belle twins muttered, "A conversation requires give-and-take amongst two or more equal parties."

The other girls laughed. Alexander and Milo merely grinned.

Back on the seventh floor, Hartleigh smiled as Katie approached the elevator. "Mother always said it's easier to ease up, than tighten up."

Katie took her arm and squeezed it. "You can always recognize an Ashley Hall girl."

"That's good, isn't it? Men know what's expected of them."

Katie punched the elevator button. Down the hall Florence Belle left her room and strolled in their direction. She, too, wore a dressing grown.

"That's all well and good in Charleston but one thing never changes: teenagers want to be with the popular kids, wear au courant clothing, smoke cigarettes, and drink beer."

"All that sounds so common."

The elevator bell rang.

"Well, before you do anything rash," cautioned Katie, "do remember that you're Tessa and Dory's guardian. Children can be trained from birth, but a ward is simply passing through your life."

The elevator doors opened, and Katie stepped aboard.

"Take what she says with a grain of salt," said Florence Belle as the doors closed. "If Katie had her way, you'd be leaving for work and dropping off your children with a babysitter. She never thinks how that may look, but it's a reflection on a husband when a woman works outside the home."

The older woman let out a long sigh. "Young people never consider consequences. I'm faced with two old maids living at home for the rest of my life. This depression has made many a young man gun-shy about starting a family."

She glanced at the elevator door. "I pleaded with my girls to select a young man, but they were too busy having fun in speakeasies or traveling to Sullivan's Island. Now they're paying the price. Our whole family will pay the price in the future."

Again, she shook her head. "I'm sorry, Hartleigh. I shouldn't put all of this on you, but there are so many single women in this town, including the ones who made the wrong decision, they're here, too, that is, after six weeks in Las Vegas for a quickie divorce. How can the institution of marriage remain sacred if you can divorce your husband after spending six weeks in Las Vegas?"

She waved this off. "Oh, don't get me started." And Florence walked away, shaking her head. "But do let me know about bridge."

Hartleigh didn't wish to pass judgment, but she couldn't understand how a woman could abandon her family for a job. Of course, widowed women like Susan needed to be out and about so they could find their next husband, but Katie was married. Why would she risk her marriage to work outside her home?

Hartleigh returned to her suite as her husband fed rounds into one Webley, then the other. Finished with each weapon, he closed the action, then checked to see that the hammer rested on an empty chamber before holstering the pistol. The twins watched from the sofa, spellbound.

"You're not to leave the hotel—understand?"

"I'm an adult, James. I believe I know what's best for me."

As her husband buttoned the leather flaps of the holsters, the twins jumped down from the sofa. "This isn't Charleston, my dear, and I don't have time to educate you this morning."

"Pardon me, but I do know how to act responsibly."

James picked up his coat and left the room, stepping across the hallway and punching the button. He returned to the open doorway where he knelt down and hugged Mary Anne first, then Little James.

"Big hug," said their father.

They hugged him tight. James Junior asked if he could have one of his father's guns and Mary Anne asked for money to buy her own purse.

"Hartleigh," said James, standing up, "though you believe you were doing the correct thing, you've actually brought our children into a war zone."

The twins attached themselves to their father's leg, a further ritual enjoyed by all. James walked stiff-legged down the hallway to the twins' bedroom where Molly waited.

Hartleigh shook her head. Whatever else she felt about James, he was a doting father. There had been that one time in Chicago when she'd walked in on Dory and Tessa lying on the bed, flanking her husband and listening to every word he had to say.

"I still don't understand why politics is so dang important," Dory had said, "but those folks really got worked up over Roosevelt being the nominee."

From the other side of the bed, Tessa raised her head. "If Uncle James believes politics is important, then it's important, and we'd better learn all about it." She turned her attention to her uncle. "I learned a great deal working for Senator Byrnes during the runoff and I want one of those floor passes for the next convention."

"Me, too," said Dory.

They both looked at Hartleigh when she came in the room. "Errol and Luke are here."

The girls sat up, glanced at each other, and then leaped off the bed. In a mirror over the dresser, hair was fluffed, plackets aligned, and cheeks pinched. Each girl then turned her back to the other so that skirts might be brushed down or blouses tucked in. That done, the two girls glanced in the mirror again, then hustled out the door, slowing to a studied walk as they left the bedroom.

"You know the rules," said Hartleigh from behind them. "Make sure the boys do, too."

James smiled. "Girls certainly are fickle."

Closing the bedroom door, Hartleigh smiled as she walked over and sat on the bed. "I'm not. I'm steadfast."

Reaching for her, James said, "I hope so because I'm still smitten."

And there occurred in that Chicago hotel room one of those interludes that made Hartleigh wonder why their relationship did not flourish in Charleston.

Down the hall Susan Moultrie came out of her room, locked the door, and hurried toward the elevator. "Morning," she said to Hartleigh.

"Good morning." In Hartleigh's opinion, Susan was showing too much cleavage, but overall her skirt and blouse were rather tame, and she did wear hose and flats.

Susan took a sheet of paper from her purse and tacked it to the wall alongside a previously posted schedule.

"What's this?" asked Hartleigh.

"The schedule for next week. People were getting confused, so each week I type it up at the senator's office; then we're all on the same schedule. Tonight we play Monopoly. Cocktail hour is at the usual time: six and downstairs in the speak."

"I thought you were a teetotaler."

"I am." She smiled. "But they serve ginger ale, and if I participate, I never have to eat in the restaurant alone."

The elevator bell rang.

Susan tapped the sheet. "Here's something you might want to remember. The Belle twins have a birthday coming up and movie night is Tuesdays."

Inside the elevator, businessmen ignored each other but checked out Susan Moultrie, and Milo smiled as James hurried out of the children's suite and down the hall. Hartleigh caught her husband's arm as he tried to board the elevator.

"Milo, my husband's jumped the gun. Catch him next time."

"Yes, ma'am."

The elevator doors closed.

"Hartleigh, I don't have time—"

Remembering last night when her husband had failed to pay a call on her boudoir, Hartleigh wrapped her arms around his neck, drew him down, and kissed him—like she'd heard the French did.

James broke this off and stumbled out of her embrace. "I . . . I don't have time for this."

She smiled warmly. "You don't have time to kiss your wife good-bye?" She patted her hair and examined her reflection in the shiny elevator doors. "Is there something wrong with me?"

"You know there's not." He cleared his throat. "But I must go to work."

"Very well. You know what's best."

Hartleigh reached over and punched the elevator button, then returned to their suite. Going through the open door, she smiled as she removed her dressing gown, letting it trail behind her like Gypsy Rose Lee. Under the gown, Hartleigh wore a very skimpy negligee.

"It's time for me to take a hot bath anyway."

Seconds later, the elevator bell rang, the doors opened, and Milo grinned . . . until he realized no passengers waited on the seventh floor, though he did hear a woman's laughter coming from the suite across the hall, one of the few times the door wasn't propped open with its cloth-covered brick.

Alexander was leaning against the hood of the Buick when James exited the lobby and hurried over.

"Women!" he muttered.

Alexander smiled, folded the newspaper, and opened the door. James slid into the backseat and the door closed behind him.

Once Alexander was behind the wheel, James said, "Sorry for the holdup."

"No problem," said the Negro. "For once, I finished the crossword."

"If you did, you cheated."

Alexander chuckled. James Stuart had to be the only white man in Washington who apologized for keeping his driver waiting, that is, his colored driver.

Later that day, an anxious front desk manager stopped Hartleigh as she crossed the lobby with Florence Belle on their way to an afternoon of bridge at Maude Byrnes's home.

"And how has been your stay so far, Mrs. Stuart?"

Hartleigh complimented the staff on their professionalism, but Florence Belle felt the turndown service came later and later and sometimes a chocolate wasn't left on their pillows.

"I'll check into that. Mrs. Stuart, might I have a word . . . ."

Florence took the hint. "I'll have one of the boys hail a cab."

"Thank you, Mrs. Belle." Once Florence had strolled away, the front desk manager said, "I'm pleased that you're enjoying your stay and we look forward to a long visit by your family here in the nation's capital. There is, however, one item on your monthly invoice I'd like to bring to your attention before it comes as a surprise to your husband."

"I thought all bills were sent to Charleston for payment."

"They are, but one item has increased significantly and I wanted to warn you about that."

"Are you speaking of charges that have been approved by my husband?"

"Well, yes and no."

"I don't understand. What exactly are we talking about?"

"Long distance telephone charges."

"Well," said Hartleigh, "there's my cousin who calls Greenville every Sunday night to speak to her family and Mrs. Moultrie who speaks to her son that same evening. My husband pays for both of those charges."

"Well, it's not those members of your party . . . ."

"Florence and Lewis Belle then?"

"Er . . . no. They are billed separately."

"Sir, I'm afraid you'll have to be more specific."

"It's your girls. They call Chicago two and three times a week, spending a good deal of time on the phone."

"Oh," said Hartleigh, nodding. "I understand. Can you have the phone removed from their bedroom?"

"I can, but there are empty bedrooms on the seventh floor from which many of these calls are placed."

"Then remove as many phones as necessary. Having a phone is a privilege not a right."

At Maude Byrnes's the conversation quickly turned to the uneasy adjustment of living in the nation's capital. Florence Belle was the most vocal, and it embarrassed Hartleigh when Florence went on and on about how much she missed Charleston and how disorienting the hubbub of Washington was.

To Hartleigh this sounded rather strange as she had visited both New York City and Chicago. Washington was just another sleepy Southern town with none of the traffic jams of Chicago or New York.

"I'm sorry, Florence," said Hartleigh, "but I find Washington fascinating . . ." Her voice trailed off as she spread her cards. Her mouth formed a small "o."

Maude Byrnes laughed. "That's a tell for sure."

"Oh, it's nothing," said Hartleigh.

"Oh, yes," said her partner, wife of "Cotton Ed" Smith, senior senator from South Carolina. Their husbands didn't get along, but that didn't stop their wives from playing bridge together. "Cotton Ed's" motto was "Cotton is king and white is supreme," which meant that during his tenure in Congress, Ed intended to keep the Negro down and the price of cotton up.

"Now, Hartleigh," teased Maude, "it's considered

bad form to slam your opponents the very first time you sit at their table."

Hartleigh didn't appear to care. She went on to execute a squeeze play that forced her opponents to discard every valuable card they held.

The trick finished, Hartleigh smiled at those at her table. "I'm sorry, but my mother says there's no such thing as social bridge."

Everyone laughed, even the ladies at the other table.

Maude said, "Nothing for you to worry about."

"You keep that up," said Maude's partner, "and you'll always be welcomed in the homes around Dupont Circle."

Across the table, "Cotton Ed's" wife wagged a finger. "Don't you dare show them any mercy. Take all tricks."

More laughter and the game proceeded until twelve tricks had been taken, then the ladies took a break to drink a little sherry and to better get to know this bridge-playing fool from Charleston.

But it was at Mamie Eisenhower's that Hartleigh's reputation was sealed. There she executed three grand slams followed by a small slam, and even another squeeze play, the cruelest play in all contract bridge.

"Who is this girl?" demanded Mrs. George S. Patton.

Sarcastically, Lloyd Fredendall's wife asked, "Play much duplicate bridge, do you?"

Later, at a party thrown by Hartleigh, George Marshall asked her husband, "How's your German, Captain Stuart?"

"Rusty," replied James.

"But your wife speaks French."

"Conversationally."

"Ever considered reenlisting? You could be posted to Paris."

"Not with the size of the army. What are we, the seventh largest army in the world?"

"But highly regarded," said Marshall. "Our army air corps is one of the best in the world. Perhaps you could take your wife on a grand tour of Europe with an emphasis on Berlin and stop by Washington on your return trip."

Why did George Marshall care? wondered James. Marshall's current responsibility was organizing the CCC for Roosevelt. Then he remembered Marshall's "little black book," in which the general kept a list of names suitable for command. Idly, James wondered where he ranked in that book.

"You're a graduate of the military academy."

"Yes, sir. Eleventh in my class."

Marshall smiled one of his rare smiles. "Well, you didn't think a pirate would place in the top ten, did you? Pirates, when all's said and done, are still sailors."

Hartleigh came out of nowhere and took Marshall by the arm. "You should be enjoying yourself, General, not letting my husband bend your ear about issues you know more about than he does."

This caused Marshall to smile again as he was led away.

"Watch yourself, General. My wife has tactics of her own."

And James stood there, observing how easily everyone mingled with each other—his wife introducing Marshall to Katie Stuart; earlier, she had introduced Lewis and Florence Belle to Patrick J. Hurley, the secretary of war; and now Hartleigh was moving on to do the honors between Ike's brother, Milton, and his wife Helen, to someone even James didn't recognize. Club Eisenhower had to be the only place in the world where politicians, diplomats, and military men mixed with such ease.

Once the party thinned out, Mamie Eisenhower said, "It appears you're settling in, Hartleigh."

"I'm learning the ropes, thanks to you and Maude Byrnes."

Hartleigh had been surprised to find that she felt more relaxed in the company of officers' wives than the circle around Maude Byrnes. Perhaps it had something to do with being married to a former officer who could give her the lay of the land.

"And the children?" asked Mamie.

"Driving the seventh floor crazy. We've been to several attractions you've recommended: the zoo and the Smithsonian, but the twins really like the mall where they can run and play."

"Well, I didn't want to overload you when we planned this party, but there are several societal dragons in this town, such as Cissy Patterson, who runs the *Washington Herald*, Alice Roosevelt Longsworth, the former first daughter of an earlier Roosevelt administration, and Walter Lippmann—people read both his column and his books. You'd do well to honor them with an invitation to your next get-together, especially if Lippmann's in town. Washington's a very small and insular town—"

"Just like Charleston," said Hartleigh with a laugh.

"But sure to grow if Mr. Roosevelt has his way. Ike says we need a dictator instead of a president, and he's said it enough times to earn the nickname 'Dictator Ike.' "

TWENTY

It was a cold and dreary day when Franklin Roosevelt arrived for his inauguration. Adding to the gloom were the soldiers manning machine guns around public buildings, the first since the Civil War. Barbed wire was rolled here and there. Sandbags protected the soldiers' positions. Across the nation, banks were either closed or limiting withdrawals. No one knew whether inauguration day would bring riot, revolution, or redemption.

In the Senate Office Building, the phone rang in Jim Byrnes's office. It was Ogden Mills, Hoover's Secretary of the Treasury, requesting that Senator Byrnes immediately come to his office.

Once they had coats and hats on, Byrnes's sister, who ran the office, opened the door, and Byrnes, a slight man, followed James out, through the crowd, and down the hallway. Sitting at a desk, opening mail, Dory Campbell bit her lip as the two men went out the door.

"Jimmy! Jimmy!" shouted the crowd.

Byrnes smiled, waved his fedora, and stayed close to Stuart, even once grabbing James's coat belt for stability. Absentmindedly, James touched his two Webleys.

Ignoring the elevators, the two men went down the marble stairs and onto the street where people clogged the sidewalks and traffic hardly moved. They had to weave their way through gawkers and job seekers, all bundled up and carrying umbrellas. The end of twelve years of Republican rule meant a lot of jobs would be opening up. Personally, James liked the snap of things.

Inside the Treasury building the air hummed with another type of excitement: banks in two of the most populous states, Pennsylvania and Massachusetts, were rumored to have closed their doors. This was premature. The banks in Pennsylvania and Massachusetts would not close until the following day.

Byrnes was immediately ushered into the treasury secretary's office where Mills tried to convince him of the necessity for a joint statement of support for the banking system from both the president and the president-elect.

"As you know, Mister Secretary," said Byrnes, "the president-elect has turned down such suggestions in the past."

"But surely someone such as yourself who has the confidence of the president-elect—"

A secretary stepped into the room. "I have Winthrop Aldrich of Chase National Bank of New York on the phone."

Mills snatched up his phone. "I need you in Washington."

Mills listened, then exploded. "Bermuda! Well, if

you go, don't buy a round-trip ticket. When you're ready to return, there'll be nothing worth returning to." He slammed down the phone.

Because of this outburst, Byrnes agreed to take Mills' proposal to FDR at the Congress Hotel.

Again FDR rebuffed the idea of any joint statement, and James got the distinct feeling that if Senator Byrnes pressed the issue, Roosevelt might just slay the messenger.

On inauguration day, James had two tickets, and Hartleigh insisted that Katie attend with him. "I'll listen on the radio."

Mary Anne pouted. "I want to go, Daddy."

James scooped her up and whirled her around. "Bugaloo, it's not for children."

"There's a parade."

"A couple of hours long, but you get to stay here with Molly and eat ice cream."

"Oh, Captain Stuart," moaned Molly, shaking her head.

Young James walked up and hit his father in the leg.

James knelt down. "Sockahoo, what've I told you about hitting?"

"Not much," commented Hartleigh, "not since you compliment him each and every time he smashes the baseball down the hallway."

Bare-headed in a drizzling rain, Roosevelt spoke for fifteen minutes, and James thought he was attending an old-fashioned revival because of the number of quotations from the Bible. During the three-hour parade that followed, everyone cheered and hollered and agreed that their country "had nothing to fear but fear itself."

The capital was on a high. The whole country was

on a high. Roosevelt would do something, anything, and if he wished to be a dictator, the American citizenry would go along with that, too.

From the inaugural ball, Katie returned to the Mayflower to call her family at the Old Maids' Club. During that phone call, she learned that one of the women who'd raised her had retired early, exhausted from listening to the day's events on the radio.

Katie hung up, bit her lip, and worried about her foster mother. She considered commandeering James's plane to make a trip to Greenville, but in the end she crossed the hall to Susan Moultrie's room, drank some wine, and discussed the possibility of Susan finding her own place in Washington before rents went sky high.

Roosevelt had insisted on austerity when it came to the inaugural, but after twelve years of Republican rule, FDR may as well been shouting into the wind. Eight thousand guests paid $5.00 per couple, all of which was donated to charity, and Dory and Tessa were among the revelers. They danced the night away with one fella after another, their dance cards always full.

Many northern Democrats mentioned to James that because of the bridge over the Cooper River, they planned to drive through Charleston on their way to Florida for their annual vacation. That was undeniably good news, but it made James feel as if he were closing a chapter on a part of his life. Could he keep his wife and babies in Washington or would they be returning to Charleston?

So James spun Hartleigh around, drank whiskey from a flask inside his coat pocket, and watched their wards whirl around the floor of the Washington Auditorium. Another two who didn't miss a dance were Lewis Belle's daughters, who danced as though their future depended on it.

James smiled down at his wife. "You have made me one happy fellow by bringing the children to Washington."

Hartleigh looked up at her husband, eyes filled with excitement. "And we're thrilled to be here."

On the return trip to the Mayflower, James teased, "Well," he said to his wards, "that's attention enough to cause any girl to forget about boys at the University of Chicago."

The girls didn't object, only issued wan smiles. They both owed their beaus letters, and in those next letters, their reports of the fun they'd had at the inaugural ball would spark a flurry of activity at the University of Chicago.

It wasn't until the following morning that James and Hartleigh learned that Elizabeth Randolph had arrived the night before and taken one of the suites down the hall. Elizabeth had been up since dawn taking stock of everything. So, as Roosevelt began his hundred-day explosion of legislation by calling Congress back into session and declaring a bank holiday, James was left to wonder how to deal with such a meddlesome woman.

Hartleigh poured her first glass of sherry for the day. "This is how I handled Mother in Charleston."

James frowned, then called his hometown. He wouldn't take this lying down.

The Stuarts weren't the only ones unhappy. It hadn't taken long for both Pearl and Molly to express their unease about Washington. In part this came from Woodrow Wilson, born and raised in the South, who had purged most of the Negroes from the federal government during his administration.

"In Charleston," said Pearl, "everybody knows their place. In Washington, white people are afraid they're gonna lose their place, so they step on people, especially the colored."

Molly agreed. "We'd be better off back home."

Tessa slept in, but Dory woke with a heightened sense of suffocation. How many handsome young men from good families had danced with her and promised that they would call at the Mayflower? And returning from the ball, several bellboys had smiled at her, one of them quite cute.

Unfortunately, all that attention could only lead to one unhappy conclusion.

On the ride up in the elevator last night, Tessa had chattered about all the boys they'd danced with, while Dory had come to the realization that she was the princess who would not feel the pea while sleeping on a stack of mattresses. Tessa was the princess who would. So the following morning, the former runaway asked if she could speak with Captain Stuart.

She left a note for Tessa explaining that someone like Errol Fiske was her choice as a husband. Errol had no family; he was on academic scholarship and worked two jobs. Dory was a survivor, too, and someone like Errol would be the man of her dreams, not one of those handsome princes from last night.

When she walked into the open-door suite, Dory interrupted a rant by Elizabeth Randolph. "I'm here, not Charleston, and you allowed the servants . . ." She became aware that someone had entered the room behind her. "Oh, hello, my dear." Elizabeth smiled. She and Dory hugged. "Did you have fun last night?" She glared at James over the girl's shoulder. "I understand they spoil you terribly, but I'm here, and we can set things right."

"May I speak with Captain Stuart?" asked Dory.

"Certainly, but are you sure you wish to burden my son-in-law with something I can, more than likely, easily help you with?"

From her chair, Hartleigh said nothing, and to Dory she appeared to have already been into the sherry. "I wish to speak with Captain Stuart alone, if you don't mind."

"Ah," said Elizabeth. "Yes." She examined James as he rose to his feet. For once, Elizabeth did not know what to say.

Hartleigh perked up. "James, why don't you take Dory into the bedroom?"

The two excused themselves and adjourned to the bedroom as Elizabeth Randolph chastised her daughter. "Must that door to the hallway always remain open? A person can't have a bit of privacy."

James took a seat on the edge of the bed and Dory pulled over the chair from the vanity. Still, she found it difficult to look James in the eye. Nervously, she glanced around.

"I've rehearsed this so many times . . . I believe this is the end of the road for me. You and your family have been wonderful to me, and I will never forget you, but it's time for me to get off this gravy train."

"What does that mean?" asked James.

"I asked Katie if there was a place for me in Jimmy Byrnes's office. Katie said that if you agreed I could open mail there six days a week."

"So, no more college."

Dory shook her head. "I've enjoyed the experience, and I thank you for the opportunity, but all of this is above my station. You, your family, and Mrs. Randolph have done so much . . . I feel as if I'm betraying you . . . the way I speak, my deportment, all my clothing . . . I owe it all to your family."

Tears started down the girl's cheeks. "But, really, all I wanted was to get off that farm. That doctor you sent me to helped me understand that I couldn't live in your world or I'd be haunted by the possibility that my past might someday intrude. But I should never be forced to return to my father's house." Now the tears began to run. "I want to work in politics. I've fallen in love with it." She rubbed away the tears.

James offered his handkerchief, and she took it.

"In all of our discussions, Dory, you've repeatedly said you wanted nothing to do with politics."

Dory straightened up. "That would've been the brat in me talking. Hopefully, I've put all that behind me."

James leaned over, took her hands, and looked into her eyes. "Dory, you're whip-smart, so, if you've gotten that chip off your shoulder, I don't see why—"

The bedroom door burst opened, and Tessa flew into the room. She saw them holding hands and rushed to Dory's side, kneeling beside the chair. Behind her, Hartleigh edged into the room and tried to blend in with the furniture. Elizabeth, however, simply walked in and demanded to know what was going on?

She was drowned out by Tessa's pleas. "Say you didn't tell him. Say you didn't."

Dory looked away. More tears rolled down her cheeks. Her hands slipped from James's.

Tessa took her friend's head in both hands and forced a sobbing Dory to face her. Tears began to run down Tessa's face, too.

"I'm . . . sorry," said Dory, "but I must go."

"No, no! I won't let you. You're my best friend, not those girls south of Broad."

Dory shook her head. "You were raised there and I'm just a farmer's daughter." She glanced at Elizabeth Randolph, who stood open-mouthed near the door. "They whisper behind my back and say the most hateful things, but up here, no one will ever know. No one will care." She wiped away more tears.

"Just tell me who these girls are," said Elizabeth, "and I'll speak with their parents."

"Don't get her hopes up," said James, standing. "You're in Washington now."

"But why didn't she bring this to me?"

Probably because the doctor had explained that trusting James would be a good step toward trusting men in general.

"But where will you stay?" asked Hartleigh. "I can't allow you to live in this city alone."

Instead of answering, Dory stood up, handed a couple of sheets of paper to James, and rushed from the room. His handkerchief went with her as she was now openly sobbing.

Tears streaming down her face, Tessa looked from one adult to another. "Do something! Stop her."

Hartleigh handed a lace handkerchief to Tessa. "First, you must calm down."

James read the sheets forced into his hand. The long and the short of it was that Dory must have James's permission to work for Jim Byrnes. A second letter vouched for Dory's character. It was signed by Major Dwight David Eisenhower of the Army Chief of Staff's office. My, my, but the girl got around.

Without a word, James left the room, and Tessa followed him, as did Hartleigh.

"What are you going to do?"

"Yes," said Tessa, blotting away tears. "I want to know."

James disappeared into his bedroom, returning to the sitting room to load his pistols. He shrugged into his holsters, his coat, and took down his fedora, and all along the way the women peppered him with plenty of questions.

"Ladies, please. Dory's my ward, and I'm duty bound to do what's best for her, but first I must think."

Tessa threw her arms around him, but very quickly, she backed away from the feel of the pistols against her chest. "Oh, thank you, Uncle James. You can do it. I know you will."

James issued a rather weak smile, then said to his wife and his mother-in-law, "If you'll excuse me."

Hartleigh could only nod. She was at a loss as to what exactly had just happened. Fathers, or in this case, uncles, were never brought into negotiations unless a final blow had to be delivered.

"What have you people done to that girl?" asked Elizabeth of her daughter. "She wasn't this spoiled when we returned from our grand tour of Europe, and there we were waited on hand and foot."

TWENTY-ONE

A decision had to be made, but James needed time to think. For this reason, he walked down seven flights of stairs, startling the bellboys when he came through the fire door.

He asked one of them to hail a cab.

As the taxi door was opened for him, the bellboy asked, "Anything wrong, Captain Stuart?" The hotel staff remained on edge whenever James was around, and not only because of the two Webleys. "Anything we can do for you?"

"Er—no, thank you." James climbed into the cab. "But thanks for asking." He flipped the young man a quarter.

"Thank you, Captain Stuart!"

The taxi took him to the small house that the Byrneses had purchased. Once James had howdied with the members of the Byrnes clan who had traveled north for the inauguration, the two men adjourned to the study to outline plans of what they might be able to accomplish with a new president.

After the men lit up a couple of Cubans, James got right to the point. "What's this Santee-Cooper project Strom Thurmond keeps promoting?"

Byrnes let out a breath of smoke. "T. C. Williams, who owns the Columbia Railway and Navigation Company, believes the creation of two lakes and one lift lock will electrify that part of the state. I agree, but it'll take persistence because the private power companies will fight it. Think about it, James. We could put thousands of people to work and, most important, bring industry and jobs to that part of the state."

"South Carolina has no money for such a project."

"That's why we must convince FDR to back this project."

"Well, he certainly owes you."

Byrnes shook his head. "That's not our ploy. We need to work hard for the president so that one day he asks 'And what do *you* need, Jim?'"

"So what the president wants is what we want. Okay, what does the president want?"

"To fix the banks, stop the foreclosures, and immediately put men to work."

"That's all?" asked James with a laugh. It sounded like so much campaign rhetoric.

"And he also wants to repeal prohibition and establish the TVA, both of which will demonstrate that the government can make a positive difference in people's lives."

"I've heard those initials bandied around. What's TVA?"

"A plan to electrify the Tennessee River Valley."

Very slowly, James nodded. "The forerunner of the Santee-Cooper project."

"You catch on fast. Ad men on Madison Avenue believe modern life has become so complicated that you begin with a simple idea and hammer it home. The president will also want to establish quotas for the amount of land farmers till and to reduce hog production. It's called domestic allotment."

James put down his cigar. "He's actually going to ask farmers to plow under crops and slaughter excess hogs when people are going without?" The long shot he'd taken in buying the Craven plantations just might pay off.

Byrnes nodded. "Most of these are Republican programs bottled up in committee, but if this new Congress doesn't play ball, FDR will call them on it. We need to live in the Senate cloakroom, James, and make sure the president's legislation is reported to the floor. When in doubt, work the cloakroom."

James pulled out Dory's letter. "And there's this I wanted to ask you about."

Byrnes smiled. "She's been bitten by the political bug. The longer Dory hung around my office, the more she saw the possibilities."

James realized he'd completely misread Dory's intentions. He thought her interest in Byrnes's office had been fueled by the number of young interns working up and down the halls of the Senate Office Building.

"She wants to drop out of school."

"Well, James, as you know, politics is only learned by doing. Still, college broadens the mind, and politics is full of people with little or no education. Dory must inoculate herself against the narrow-minded. I will recommend a course of study for her as my father-in-law once did for me."

"She wants to move out and pay her own way."

Byrnes nodded. "I'll keep that in mind when I hire her full-time."

"Jim, you can't really believe that Dory should live on her own in Washington, can you?"

"I think it speaks well of Dory." Byrnes paused. "I take it she had a rough childhood."

Jim Byrnes knew hardship firsthand. His father had died when he was six and his mother had supported the family by dressmaking. Mrs. Byrnes had become so proficient in making dresses for those living south of Broad that she'd been able to afford her own home there. Still, that didn't mean Jim mixed with those living south of Broad. Everyday, he had to earn their reluctant approval.

James explained. "Dory was the only girl in the family and when her mother passed, she was pressed into service for her three brothers and her father. After an older brother joined the navy, Dory ran away to Charleston where my sister found her and brought her home. The girl had no manners, little education, and a dreary outlook about the future. Several girls, including my wife, cleaned her up, dressed her up, and put her to work in the kitchen. Every afternoon Dory had a session with a tutor. That was Elizabeth Randolph's idea."

"Lucky girl."

"Here in Washington, I paid for her to see a psychologist. Frankly, I was tired of her chip-on-the-shoulder attitude, and those sessions were one of the terms of her becoming my ward. Lewis Belle drew up the contract."

Byrnes smiled. "You made her sign a contract?"

"We all signed: me, my wife, and Tessa, who was already my ward because my brother was continually at sea and Tessa wished to travel across state lines with my family."

Byrnes sat back in his chair. "You know, the White House pays more money than a senator for opening mail."

"Really? You think Dory could work there?"

Byrnes smiled. "Let me make a call. The White House has been inundated with mail for the new president."

That night, when he returned from work, James called the seventh floor from a house phone in the lobby. "Susan, this is James. Could you please join me in the speak?"

"Are you sure that's a good idea?"

"If I wanted someone to drink with, I'd call my wife."

Susan said it would be a few minutes and for James to order a sandwich or he was going to be drunk before she arrived. James did as she asked, and Susan ordered a ginger ale when the waiter seated her.

"What's this all about?" she asked.

James appeared to be tight so Susan also ordered coffee.

"You know," said James, looking around, "there's a lot of single women in this speak."

"Yes, and you appear to be trolling."

"What?" He looked at her. "What do you mean?"

"You wear no wedding band."

James glanced at his hand. "I don't wear jewelry. I'm not a girl."

"Well," said Susan, "Washington is a hotbed of intrigue, and if you don't wear a wedding band, you're fair game."

"But I have a wife."

Susan chuckled. "And that broke my heart."

"Oh, come on, Susan. I'm ten years older than you."

"When I was ten," she said, continuing to grin, "you promised to wait for me."

"I was being silly, just playing along."

"I wasn't."

The ginger ale and coffee arrived, and the plate with the crumbs from the sandwich was whisked away. Susan sipped from her glass and James from his cup.

"They make good coffee here."

"James, quit stalling."

He put down his cup. "I simply want to know how things are coming along."

"If you mean the job—fine. If you're asking whether I miss my boy or not, I've finagled a position as Byrnes's personal secretary when he returns to South Carolina." She put down her glass. "You know, those two are the sweetest couple."

"They don't have any children."

"And I'm truly sorry for them." A wistful look crossed her face. "I'd like to have more."

James's face reddened. "Susan, you are treading dangerously close to the line here."

"Oh, silly, I'm no home wrecker." Still a coy smile crossed her face. "But I do have suitors."

"Uh-huh." James reached for his pen. "Just give me their names and I'll have them checked out."

She sat up. "You'll do no such thing. Besides, you're already a problem."

"Me? What did I do?"

Susan studied her glass. "I should move out. Be on my own."

"You, too? Dory said the same thing."

"Which I can understand. You make it too easy, and if I don't leave soon, I'll become another of your dependents."

James gave her a blank stare.

She leaned into the table and lowered her voice. "Someone has to take care of me to have his babies. Daddy could've fixed me up with an apartment, even a house, but I'd never been on my own."

"Why is it you modern girls need to be so independent?"

She laughed. "Not me. I want a man at my beck and call."

"Good. Not the beck and call bit, but you should remarry."

"I can't if I continue to live under your roof."

He shook his head. "I don't understand."

"Some boy comes along, I fall for him, and then he learns I live with you on the seventh floor."

"But you're safe up there."

"James, no girl wants to be that safe." She drank more ginger ale. "I'm a princess locked up in your tower. I need to be rescued."

James waved this off. "Aw, don't be so silly."

"Katie and Tessa aren't worried, but who am I to you?"

"Really?" He studied her face. "This is a problem?"

Susan smiled and nodded.

"Okay then. Let me ask you this: How do you get along with Dory Campbell? I've just gotten a job for her opening mail in the White House. You two might live together. Hartleigh could even help you pick out the boarding house."

Susan laughed. "Oh, James, that's what I mean. You don't think I haven't learned a trick or two since I've been in Washington? Remember, my name used to be 'Susan Chase,' and we Chase girls have always been known for our self-reliance."

TWENTY-TWO

A few days later, Eileen and Royce Craven stepped off the Palmetto Special in Washington. Their round-the-world honeymoon had only fueled Eileen's interest in traveling. Her husband agreed, not because a happy wife made a happy life, but the constant motion would make his new bride forget all about her former husband, a colorful personality in his own right.

After giving her son a peck on the cheek, and Royce shaking his hand, Eileen asked, "What? No servants?"

"I was abandoned by Alexander. He's living the sweet life south of Broad with little or no responsibility. Elizabeth Randolph has moved in with us."

His mother arched an eyebrow. "Need help there?"

"Desperately. Hartleigh stays soused all the time."

"I'll see what I can do."

"Then join my mother-in-law and me for breakfast tomorrow morning. I'll leave a wakeup call."

"Oh, my dear," said Eileen, taking her son's arm, "don't tell me you breakfast with Elizabeth Randolph every morning."

"It gives Hartleigh a chance to sober up from all the sherry she drank the night before." When they looked at him, puzzled, James explained, "The sherry softens her mother's constant fault finding."

"Elizabeth's lonely, James."

"Mother, you're sympathizing with the wrong side here."

The following morning, the four of them met in the restaurant for breakfast. Katie Stuart did not join them, even though she sometimes gave cover to James. Instead, she snatched a bagel, smeared it with cream cheese, and headed off to the office.

"A bagel?" asked Eileen. "What's that?"

"A hard donut," explained Elizabeth. "It's so bland you must spread something on it, usually cream cheese."

"I know what cream cheese tastes like," said Royce, "and I'm not sure that's much of an improvement."

After their plates were removed, Eileen asked, "Well, how's the social life in Washington?"

"Ask Florence Belle. I don't care to attend parties unescorted."

His mother turned her sights on her son and asked, "James, have you not found a suitable escort for your mother-in-law?"

Royce cut in. "I can't believe a woman as attractive as you is not spoken for."

Elizabeth smiled. "Thank you, Royce, but I have too many responsibilities to consider romance."

"You don't mean that," said Eileen. "Every woman considers romance."

"I don't like the direction this conversation is taking," said James. "I can vouch for my mother-in-law. She is a good and decent woman."

Nodding and smiling, Elizabeth said, "Thank you, James."

"We're all good persons, but when a fellow shows some interest—"

"I hope I did more than that," said Royce with a laugh. "You made me wait a considerable period of time."

"Well," said Eileen, blushing, "it was only right."

"People, please," pleaded James, looking everywhere but at his mother.

Royce leaned toward his wife. "Just who did I beat out for your affections?"

"Oh, Royce, a lady never kisses and tells."

"Who did you kiss?" He straightened up. "I may wish to call on them."

"Oh, silly you, you flatter me." Turning serious, Eileen said to Elizabeth, "I haven't had a good game of bridge since you and Hartleigh left Charleston."

"Then we must arrange one. There are some very good bridge players in Washington."

"Good," said Eileen, "it'll put Charleston out of my mind."

"Put Charleston out of your mind? Why would you want to do that? Your wedding is one of my fondest memories of last spring."

At this, Royce and James excused themselves.

"Really, James," said his mother-in-law. "Smoking so early?" She turned to Eileen. "I try to look out for these children, but James's bedroom door is left wide open all night."

"I'm sure he's only looking out for you and the girls."

"And since Molly left, James makes the children sleep in their own bedrooms. Why, even the new nanny sleeps in the children's sitting room. James had a portable bed brought it."

"Oh, Elizabeth," said Eileen, "all of these young people think they know what's best. Sooner or later, they'll come to their senses."

"Well," said Elizabeth, leaning over the table, "that marriage is in trouble, and I'm worried about it."

Eileen dismissed her concerns with a wave of the hand. "I'm sure you're worried about nothing."

"Then why do I find my daughter in the sherry all the time?"

"Oh, my dear," said Eileen, chuckling, "don't you know their generation drinks and smokes in excess. They go out every night and stay out late. They think it makes them hip. I think that's the word they use." Eileen paused. "Now, do you want to know the latest gossip from Charleston or not?"

"Yes. Please, tell all."

Eileen's gossip included a daughter sent to Spartanburg before she began to show; then there was the very prominent young man who was caught climbing out of another young man's bedroom window in the middle of the night; and the rumor of two families, who behind closed doors were swapping mates.

"You know," said Eileen with a chuckle, "I do believe that if divorce was legal in South Carolina, those couples would not fess up to their spouse-swapping parties or change partners."

"Yes," agreed Elizabeth, laughing, "both couples date back to Ashley Hall and Charleston's Boys' High School. They've known each other since birth."

Elizabeth's tone changed. "But tell me, what's so disappointing about Charleston?" She glanced at the restaurant bar where James and Royce Craven smoked cigars. "I wouldn't want the children to know, but I desperately miss home."

"It's the Negroes, my dear. They seem to think this Roosevelt character gives them a pass on their work."

"My word, what do you mean?" The unofficial motto of the low country was to never give the Negro a leg up.

"Can I make it any plainer? They're lazy." She gestured to where James stood at the bar. "I miss a strong hand to guide them."

"But certainly you have Royce."

"Oh," said Eileen, shaking her head, "Royce wants everyone to like him, even the Negroes. You should see how Alexander and Pearl run your household. They've made themselves quite at home."

Since Elizabeth Randolph was a glass-half-empty type of person, she could easily believe the Negroes in her employ were roaming her home and doing as they pleased. It made her shiver, and with three straight mornings of similar conversation, Elizabeth was soon on a train back to Charleston.

"Poor Alexander," commented James as he, his wife, his mother, and Royce saw Elizabeth off at Union Station, "he'll never forgive me."

His mother gripped his arm. "If there's anyone who knows how to play the game, it's Alexander." Releasing his arm, Eileen added, "But as close as you two are, it's probably best you telegraph him."

Katie was with Jim Byrnes the morning FDR called the senator to the White House. There, Roosevelt explained that he would treat all reporters the same and have no special relationship with any particular reporter, as had President Hoover and the presidents before him. All reporters would be invited to twice-weekly press conferences.

"How does that sounds to you, Mrs. Stuart, you being a former reporter?"

"Sir," said Katie, "if there was only one reporter who had your ear, and that reporter was me, I would prefer the old system, but if you're intent on holding conferences with all reporters in attendance, I'd immediately resign from Senator Byrnes's office and accept the *Piedmont's* offer to cover the White House."

"Then," said the president with a sly smile, "you'd be out of luck. That first press conference begins in twenty minutes."

Katie glanced at her boss. "The senator will have my resignation in less than ten."

Roosevelt looked at Byrnes. "Sorry about this, Jim."

But Roosevelt didn't look very sorry.

Missy LeHand, Roosevelt's girl Friday, scrounged up an extra steno pad, and when Katie returned from the powder room, Missy held out a phone.

"Bony Pearce from Greenville. He's pleased to have you aboard once again."

Minutes later, the Secret Service stopped Katie as she tried to reenter the Oval Office. "Sorry, but you're not cleared for this."

Missy Lehand reached around Katie, and using a safety pin, attached a small sheet of paper to her left jacket lapel. It read:

Mrs. Catherine Stuart
The Piedmont
Greenville, South Carolina

"Very good," said the agent and he escorted Katie into the Oval Office where a scrum of male reporters made way and Katie ended up in one of the few chairs near the president's desk.

Roosevelt laughed. "Gone over to the enemy, have you, Mrs. Stuart?"

When the other reporters appeared puzzled, the president had Katie stand and face them. After Robert Trout of CBS Radio read LeHand's note out loud for the benefit of those in the rear of the room, the reporters broke into spontaneous applause.

"I thought you said no favorites, Mister President," quipped Trout.

Roosevelt chuckled. "Well, maybe one or two."

In Katie's family, this story was passed down from generation to generation, and upon her death, the hastily scribbled credential was found in Katie's personal Bible.

After the press conference ended, a conference that dealt with questions ranging from banking and agriculture to foreign policy, FDR asked Byrnes, "Well, Jim, how'd I do?"

"Quite admirably, Mister President. I'm not mentally agile enough to be able to leap from one topic to another." Byrnes was too much the gentleman to mention that FDR's hands now trembled and somewhere along the line, he'd broken out in a cold sweat.

"And when your sons came in to say their goodbyes before returning to Groton—that was a nice touch."

After Royce and Eileen moved on to New York to see a few shows, Franklin Belle and his wife, Georgiana, arrived in the capital, took a room on the seventh floor, and spent a good bit of time with Lewis and his wife, Florence. They played bridge, drank liquor, and reminisced about the way the world used to be.

Franklin had escorted Georgiana to the nation's capital at the insistence of Florence Belle so Florence could have a friendly face around. Back home, Florence and Georgiana hadn't been all that close, simply additional members of the Belle clan.

Lewis understood his wife's concerns. In Charleston, she knew who was who, but in Washington she became stymied by her own social code. For example, Dwight David Eisenhower, son of a farmer, and his wife, Mamie, daughter of a Denver businessman, entertained regularly at the Willard Hotel and invited just about everyone in official Washington to join them. Florence could not figure out whether she and her husband should attend. Though Eisenhower worked in the office of the chief of staff of the army and everyone said he was an ambitious swell, Eisenhower was a mere major.

At cocktails one evening on the seventh floor, Franklin Belle announced to the assembled personage that he had come to Washington to watch "this Roosevelt person destroy the republic."

A hush fell over the gathering. Everyone in the room was a Roosevelt Democrat, and they knew, because of the interview requests received from reporters, that the days of small-town Washington were over. Something big was about to happen, and they did not believe that the republic would be destroyed.

Lewis clapped Franklin on the shoulder. "Well, hang onto your hat, cousin, because the next few months will astound you."

Unbeknownst to the general public, the Hoover people still came to work each day and toiled alongside the Roosevelt people to revive the economy. And James found it comforting that with all the vilifying of Republicans in the last election, there were still people who put country first.

That went for the ordinary Joes, too. All kinds of schemes poured into the White House as to how to end this depression, one being that the country should go off the gold standard and allow the currency to inflate. This suggestion had been slowly gaining momentum when the Franklin Belles arrived with pictures of their new grandchild.

"Not that the boy has any future with these communists running the government. Farmers will become so dependent on that dole that they'll never work hard again."

Whenever anyone raised the issue of plowing crops under and slaughtering pigs, James tried to imagine how large a check the government would soon be sending him. Landlubber politics had turned out to be very profitable for the House of Stuart.

Full of himself, James asked Franklin, Senior, if he objected to the CCC taking unemployed young men off the streets and having them plant trees in the national forests.

"Of course, I object. Over three million dollars is to be poured into that boondoggle. There aren't enough projects to absorb three million dollars, so where's that money really going?" The older man flashed a wicked grin. "A million dollars here, a million there, and soon you're talking some real money."

It was then that James realized that Franklin Belle was no novice when it came to a good, sound economic argument, and it reminded James that even Franklin Roosevelt didn't completely buy into public works projects. Roosevelt thought it took too long for public works money to impact people's lives, but the unemployed could join the CCC and start planting trees next week and receiving a paycheck the following week.

Still, Franklin Belle did not relent. "Your friend Roosevelt wants to give relief to the state and local governments. I don't know of a state or local relief effort that's not totally corrupt. And your boy should know. Tammany Hall helped elect him governor."

"Mister Belle," argued James, "you seem to have a rather negative view of public service."

"Shouldn't I? You're asking business to compile codes and determine hours and wages. That means the big boys will become monopolists, and with the government behind their codes and wages, prices will rise. Now, where does that get us? Perhaps it's best if we simply leave the economy alone and let it recover on its own." Belle took a swallow of his bourbon. "By the way, Captain Stuart, does Roosevelt have any businessmen in his so-called 'brain trust'?"

Invited downstairs to the hotel's speak, Hartleigh met several of Katie's friends from the Senate Office Building, easily the best place to work in Washington. The building had steam heat, lavatories with hot and cold running water, and telephones. The building was connected to the Capitol by an underground passageway.

Nina had grown up in Brooklyn; Addy in Columbus, Ohio; and Edna in upstate New York. After exchanging pleasantries, they got down to business, that is, until some young man showed an interest in one of them.

"Did you hear the president last night?" asked Addy from Columbus.

Everyone had. Restaurants had emptied, traffic had stopped, and movies played to empty theaters. Even the Stuart twins had gone down easily, lying in bed clutching their teddy bear or Raggedy Ann as the new nanny sat riveted to what Franklin Roosevelt said about banking in his first fireside chat.

Hartleigh knew little about banks, their operation being the bailiwick of her husband, but the president had patiently explained that banks did not keep deposits in their vaults; they put that money to work keeping the wheels of industry and agriculture turning. FDR went on to explain that in the last few days of February and the first days of March, a general rush by a large portion of the population to turn their bank deposits into currency or gold—a rush so great that even the soundest banks couldn't raise enough cash to meet the demand—meant that by the afternoon of March third, scarcely a bank in the country was open.

"It was then," he said, "that I proclaimed a national bank holiday so as to reconstruct our financial and economic system, but still allow its depositors, meaning you, the general public, to be able to withdraw enough money for food and household necessities and for businesses to make their payrolls. This bank holiday, while resulting in great inconvenience for all, is affording an opportunity to supply just enough currency to meet the situation."

"But he's not going to open all the banks," argued Nina from Brooklyn.

"Eventually," said Hartleigh. When no one spoke, she glanced around the table. "Oh, I'm sorry. Did I speak out of turn?"

It would appear no one cared. "Aren't some of those banks insolvent?" asked Amy.

Again, Hartleigh glanced around the table while Katie stared, open-mouthed. This was a Hartleigh she'd never seen before.

"I guess so," said Hartleigh, "but to hear the president, all the banks will be open by the end of the month, and the treasury will back them through the Federal Reserve."

"Well," said Addy, grinning, "I hope they have enough money. Hoover gave ninety million dollars to Central Republic Bank—it was too large to fail—and it sank without a trace."

Everyone knew the story of Central Republic

Bank of Chicago. Word of its collapse had spread, fueling even more withdrawals.

Nina chuckled. "Still, I'll bet the bankers got *their* money out."

"And turned it into gold," agreed Katie, nodding.

Edna laughed. "Daddy says bankers always get their share."

"Well, that's because there's always a big-shot politician associated with every bank."

"Why does that not surprise me?" asked Katie.

All of them laughed.

"There was something about the banks being certified by the Treasury," suggested Nina, turning serious again. "I didn't know the government had enough auditors to evaluate every single bank in the country."

"State banks are excluded," said Hartleigh, speaking up again. "That'll cut down on the examiners' work." Hartleigh felt a surge of pride that she could hold her own among these clever girls and all because she could ask James anything. Most husbands would snap at their wives that banking and politics were none of their business.

Hartleigh understood there was women's work and men's work, but it was nice if your husband explained how the world worked, and in Washington, there was a great deal to explain.

"Hartleigh!"

"What?" She looked at Katie.

"You drifted off."

"But you were smiling," said Addy, "so it must've been a pleasant daydream."

"Yes," asked Nina, "were you dreaming of Robert Taylor?"

More laughter.

Hartleigh felt the heat run up her neck. "I'm so very sorry."

Across the table, Nina shook her head. "What a shame to waste all those smarts on raising a bunch of kids."

"Nina!" shouted the other girls.

"Shame on you!" said one of them.

"Yes," concurred Katie, "Hartleigh's my guest."

"I'm sorry," said Nina, "but I'm from Brooklyn and we—"

"Oh, yes," said Edna, "we can hear that in your voice."

Nina glared at her. "You people from upstate—"

"We all choose our path in life," said Addy. "One path is not necessarily superior to the other."

"I'm sorry, but I disagree," said Nina. "I have an invalid mother and a no-account husband who rummages through my purse whenever I'm not looking." Straightening up in her chair, she finished. "I'm the superior woman because I care for a family and go to work every day."

Katie said, "That sounds rather bitter."

"You've got that right. My husband wasn't an alcoholic when we married, but this depression has broken him. It's not right for a man not to have a job. The only reason I have *my* job is because Daddy supported FDR instead of Al Smith in the face of Tammany Hall opposition."

"Do you think your husband will ever stop his drinking?" asked Hartleigh.

Nina's eyes iced over as she stared at the woman across the table. "And why would you make my personal life your business?"

Hartleigh looked into her lap. In a low voice, she said, "I just thought James might be able to help find a job for your husband."

Nina stared at Hartleigh, then her face scrunched up in pain and she burst into tears. Without a word, she bolted for the ladies' room. People in the speakeasy stopped and stared at them.

Katie pushed back her chair. "Please excuse me."

Abby and Edna soon followed. Hartleigh was left sitting at the table, and glancing around, she saw people, heads together, whispering and staring at her.

Hartleigh smiled, got to her feet, and returned to the seventh floor. She didn't belong with those career girls. She belonged with her family, and she belonged with her husband, so after dressing in a skimpy nightgown and liberally spraying herself with perfume, she joined James in his bed. Or perhaps she did so to solidify her position in life.

"Did you close the doors?" asked James taking her into his arms.

"And locked them, so I can make as much noise as I care to."

TWENTY-THREE

The president requested that the House agricultural committee come to the Oval Office. There he read them the riot act. He wanted the Farm Credit Administration Act and its companion legislation, the Home Owners Loan Act, reported out of committee and voted on. "These are desperate times that require swift action."

The following day, the Agricultural Adjustment Act was sent to the White House for Roosevelt's signature. In a follow-up conversation, FDR asked George Peek to run the agency.

"Mister President," said Peek, "you know I'm opposed to central planning."

"Only because you believe this agency will become another government bureaucracy, but by taking this job, George, you'll be present at the creation. It'll be as bureaucratic as you allow it."

Peek signed on.

Next up, the CCC.

The Civilian Conservation Corps was opposed by labor because its low wages undermined the closed shop.

"Utter rubbish," the president told the leaders of the unions. "The CCC will employ a mere quarter of a million people. Fourteen million people are unemployed. Besides, we'll put a union man in charge."

So the unions signed on, and the Bonus Army disappeared from the streets of Washington, as did James Stuart's Webleys.

Then Roosevelt took on the Volstead Act, and the Beer and Wine Act passed in one day, actually, in one afternoon. It would take three-quarters of the states to repeal the Eighteenth Amendment (passed later that year), but prohibition was effectively dead, and when the first case of Buds rolled off the assembly line in St. Louis, a team of Clydesdale horses, pulling a beer wagon, delivered those Budweisers to the most famous "wet" in the country, former governor of New York, Al Smith.

Leaving the Senate Office Building, James told Susan Moultrie that he had to drop off something, so they moved from that modern marvel to a down-at-the-heels building off the mall.

"By the way," she said, "I'll be taking Dory to look at apartments tomorrow."

James glanced at her as he pushed open the door of the decrepit building. "Hartleigh's not joining you?"

Susan chuckled. "James, I don't think you appreciate how much your wife's caught up in the Washington social scene. This afternoon she's having high tea with Alice Roosevelt Longworth. If your wife survives that, she'll be admitted into Washington's inner circle, something Alice might do just to spite Cissy Patterson, managing editor of the *Washington Herald.*"

Susan followed James across a lobby where paint peeled from the walls and disinfectant barely masked the odor of mildew and stale tobacco.

"What is this place?" asked Susan.

"The Federal Security Building, but we won't be here long."

"What do they do here?"

"Doesn't matter. The real brains of the outfit is upstairs."

"Who's that?"

"Harry Hopkins. FDR dragooned him down here from Albany, and I understand Hopkins took a cut in pay to handle federal relief."

"Good God, but he must be busy. Will he have time to see us?"

James laughed as they stepped into the elevator. "Kiddo, you won't be able to miss him."

When they stepped off the elevator, their footsteps and a series of banging heating pipes echoed down the uncarpeted hallway.

In the middle of the hall sat a figure at a desk scribbling on a stack of Western Union telegrams. Susan could barely make out the man enveloped in smoke and appearing to have more than one person lined up at his desk. After three years of depression, all sources of relief had dried up, and even those who hated big government were calling for the new president to assume dictatorial powers before America went the way of Italy or Germany.

They stood in front of the desk until Hopkins looked up.

"Ah, Captain Stuart, and what can I do for you?"

Cigarette ash covered the front of Hopkins's suit,

he had circles under his eyes, and his tie was askew. In front of Hopkins lay piles of yellow paper: Western Union telegrams with names, addresses, and, where possible, telephone numbers on them.

James passed his own list across the cluttered desk. "Senator Byrnes asked that you consider these people."

"From South Carolina, I would imagine."

"Actually, many of the names are from Grinnell, Iowa." Grinnell, Iowa, was Harry Hopkins's hometown.

Hopkins stopped smiling. "Who put you up to this?"

"Sir, I've worked for the senator for the last three years and I can vouch for his integrity. Byrnes, like you, always looks out for the little guy—no matter where he might live. If the senator chooses to make a point with these names, it's for good reason."

Hopkins nodded. "Very well." And he put Byrnes's list on the top of the pile.

To Susan the whole scene was surreal. She'd heard that Roosevelt did not want deficit spending, but Frances Perkins, the first woman in a president's cabinet, had enlisted strong Senate support, demanding public relief for millions of Americans.

Roosevelt had finally given in and endorsed deficit spending, but only because he knew Harry Hopkins would demand that those receiving government assistance be put to work.

"Thank you, Mister Hopkins."

"No, Captain Stuart, thank you." He looked at Susan. "You, too, Mrs. Moultrie."

Susan walked away, stunned. "He knows me? How does someone from a relief agency in upstate New York know me?"

James clapped her on the shoulder as they returned to the elevator. "Everyone in Washington knows their allies. They know their enemies even better."

When the elevator doors opened, reporters and several photographers rushed off and down the hall. James gripped Susan around the waist and pulled her out of the way. The reporters did not stop, nor did they apologize, but made straight for Hopkins's desk in the middle of the hallway. Hopkins greeted them with a snarl.

Undeterred, the reporters demanded answers and cameras flashed away. Where there was smoke, there was fire, and where money was being given away, there was always graft.

Over the hubbub, they heard Hopkins raise his voice. "I'm not going to last six months here, so I'll do as I please."

After Susan adjusted the placket of her dress, she smiled nervously at James, and then they joined a group of young men with their own handfuls of Western Union telegrams. Going down in the elevator, the young men stared straight ahead, waiting for the doors to open and infused with the righteousness of their cause.

Before the doors opened, Susan turned to James. "Is it true what the newspapers say, that Harry Hopkins, in his first two hours on the job, gave away over two million dollars?"

"Believe it!" said more than one of the young men who gripped telegrams in their hands.

"Yes, sirree," said the elevator operator. "Someone's finally come to Washington who's not afraid of the Big Bad Wolf."

A few days later, James called his brother-in-law at the Stuart and Company warehouse in Charleston.

"The winds of change—they are a blowing."

"I've applied for the Anheuser-Busch franchise for Charleston, Columbia, and Greenville," said

Edmund Hall. "We may be in a weaker position in Columbia, but your cousin's got Greenville and I've secured Charleston for us."

"Sounds like you're going to live more comfortably than any engineer in Boulder City."

Edmund laughed. "As long as I can keep your sister happy. Look, James, Billy Ray and I want to take our wives to New York to see a few Broadway shows. What do you think? Can I get away for a week or two?"

"You and Billy Ray?"

"Yes." Edmund laughed. "The marriage of your mother to Billy Ray's father makes us all brothers."

"Then do as you wish," said James, unable to comprehend this relationship.

"Oh, come on, James, there're no hard feelings. We both beat the other bloody and our wives were thrilled with the results."

"Well, if Grace Craven and Sue Ellen Hall can bury the hatchet, then there's hope for me and my mother-in-law."

Again Edmund laughed. "Sorry, James, but I've met your mother-in-law and that relationship is beyond repair."

Next, James called Christian Andersen, who was more difficult to reach since there were no phone booths in the cotton or rice fields of the low country. James left word at his house on High Battery.

When Christian returned his call, James said, "I have all these memos. It sounds as if you're making real headway with all the planting that you're *not* doing."

"It's strange. I've never been paid for not working, but I've created a stock rotation plan that'll bring all your land under the plow, just at different times. I barely got the pig farms established before I received a letter telling me to limit that production, too. Funny, isn't it? When I left the farm, I vowed I'd never return."

"This is a different kind of farming. Instead of manure, we fertilize our crops with politics."

Christian laughed. "In those fields taken out of production, I'm placing tenants and sharecroppers. Personal-use land is not subject to the same rules as larger farmers. And I'm stockpiling fertilizer. The overseer at Cooper Hill says the trick to managing those AAA programs will be to take the poorest-producing acreage out of production and heavily fertilize the rest. He may be right. The feed and seed stores stay sold out of fertilizer."

"What's this about schoolteachers?"

"Stuart and Company now employs two school-teachers, one black and one white, who teach the three R's so that my tenants and croppers can read the instructions on, say, a sack of fertilizer."

"Well," said James, chuckling, "enjoy it as long as it lasts. There's no way an exclusive tax on companies processing farm products can be constitutional. It's like the government giving a rebate to farmers. The special interest groups will take this all the way to the Supreme Court if they have to."

"Speaking of politics, the white power structure has been severely rattled by that Agricultural Adjustment Act. Many Negroes cast the first votes of their lives when asked to determine what marketing quotas to adopt for cotton and tobacco. Since you needed a two-thirds vote to determine those quotas, white farmers went farm to farm, encouraging Negroes to vote."

James laughed. "And during the next election, they'll find some way to suppress the black vote. How's the family?"

"Jonathan's talking, but he doesn't understand enough words to express himself. We still have a lot of finger pointing and screaming. Rachel simply gives up and turns the boy over to his nanny. Oh, by the way, Rachel's pregnant again."

"Well, unless you have twins, the Andersens will never catch up with the Stuarts."

"You're not going to win this one, James. The Belles run to twins. Jonathan was the exception. By the way, making babies is not only fun, but it can become a genuine engineering project."

"Come again?"

"Ever heard of the rhythm method? Catholics use it to avoid pregnancy, but as I explained to Rachel, it could be used in reverse to produce a litter of children. I'll send you some charts."

Katie Stuart walked into the open-door suite, glanced at the bedroom being used by James, and knocked on the opposite door.

"Come in!"

In the bedroom, Hartleigh was at her vanity, examining herself in the mirror. She wore a bra and panties and her dressing gown was pulled back but not off her shoulders.

"I never did like the idea of wrapping my chest to flatten it." She glanced at her bosom. "I guess I'm simply too well-endowed. Anyway, James likes the new style."

Hartleigh wheeled around on her stool and faced Katie, who had taken a seat on the corner of the bed. Hartleigh pulled tight her dressing gown and robed it.

"I don't know what to say. When we returned to the table, you were gone."

"Well, people were staring . . . ."

"And we're sorry for putting you in such a position. Nina wants to apologize."

"There's nothing to apologize for. I said something

that upset her. I should be the one apologizing."

"I think you should know that Nina called this morning. When she went home, she and her mother stood her husband under a cold shower until he sobered up, then they poured coffee into him, followed by plenty of ham and eggs. He's downstairs, waiting for James in the lobby."

Hartleigh clapped her hands. "Oh, goody!"

"Nina told him if he botches this, they're finished."

Hartleigh frowned. "Isn't that a bit harsh?"

"There are plenty of women in this town who wish they were home raising their kids, but their families need the money."

"I'm sorry to hear that."

"Anyway," said Katie, shrugging, "they'd like you to join us tonight and let us make it up to you."

"Oh, Katie, that's so nice, but I realized I don't fit in with your crowd." She continued to smile. "Anyway, I'm going to be busy in the evenings. I'm trying to get pregnant again."

Later that day when Hartleigh found Mary Anne playing with her dolls but could not find her son, she went looking for him in her husband's bedroom. Lying on the bed were James's Webleys, and standing on a chair was her son rummaging through the chest of drawers. Hartleigh raced across the room, grabbed the back of the boy's shirt, and pulled him off the chair. Young James squealed as he was placed on the floor.

Hartleigh spun the boy around. "What do you think you're doing? This is not your room."

Nonplussed, young James said, "Bullets for gun."

Hartleigh glanced at the Webleys. "And what were you planning to do with the bullets if you found them?"

The child became indignant. "Bullets fire gun."

Hartleigh headed for her husband's closet. "I'll

light a fire under you." Jerking down a belt, she gestured at the closet as she returned to where young James stood. "As far as bullets are concerned, you'll need the combination to the safe."

The following day Susan Moultrie took Dory Campbell and Tessa Stuart to the Capitol Hill location of National Capital Bank to open their own checking accounts. National Capital Bank had been serving the Capitol Hill area since 1893 and would continue to pay dividends throughout the Great Depression.

"This is the kind of bank where you want to deposit your hard-earned money." Susan gestured around the spacious lobby with its long wooden counters and long lines at each teller window. "It's very conservative."

"Mrs. Moultrie," called out a white-haired gentleman who walked over to greet them. "What brings you in?"

Susan shook hands with the older man while Tessa and Dory gave modified curtsies.

"Mister Didden," said Susan, "I can't imagine why the big boss would be working in the lobby."

"After the new President's fireside chat, depositors have lined up at our windows to redeposit their money. It's quite amazing." He turned to the teenagers. "And who might these young ladies be?"

"Ashley Hall graduates from Charleston. Tessa Stuart's attending Georgetown University and Dory Campbell works in the White House answering mail. The president receives over seven thousand letters each week."

Dory smiled and nodded.

"Tessa studies business at Georgetown and works weekends." Susan smiled. "Well, the weekends when the boys leave her alone. She answers mail in Senator Byrnes's office when she has the time."

"So they'll both have regular paychecks."

"And need checking accounts to pay their bills."

"Will you be signing on the accounts, Mrs. Moultrie?"

"I will." Susan drew two envelopes from her purse. "Captain James Stuart is the girls' legal guardian. If you need to speak with him, he'll make himself available."

"That won't be necessary. Captain Stuart also banks here." Didden gestured toward one of the desks. "Let's go see Michael."

A half hour later, both girls were the proud owners of individual checking accounts having fifty dollars in each.

On their way out of the bank and through the lobby doors, Tessa asked, "I can write my own checks?"

"Have you seen how it's done?" asked Susan.

Tessa nodded. "Uncle James had me pay some bills at Nana's house and Nana signed them. They were the first checks I'd ever filled out and some of the first checks Nana had ever signed. Grampa always paid the bills."

"We live in a different world, as your Uncle James understands, and we girls must know how to protect ourselves."

"Protect ourselves?" asked the girls in unison.

Dory glanced back at the bank.

Susan took their arms and all three continued down Pennsylvania Avenue. "The only rule of money that a girl needs to know is that if you have money, you're free. If you have no money, you'll fall into some man's orbit."

"That's bad?" questioned Tessa. "Don't all girls want to marry and have babies?"

"Of course, but look what happened to me. My Artie was killed while building the bridge over the

Cooper River. I was lucky I had friends and relatives to fall back on, but not every girl's so fortunate."

Dory nodded. She knew exactly what Susan Moultrie meant. Money equaled freedom.

"So it's important for a girl to always have money. Now," added Susan, "we need to find an apartment for Dory and me."

"May I go along?" asked Tessa. "Perhaps Uncle James will agree to me having my own apartment."

"Not a good idea while you're still in school. Does Hartleigh put any restrictions on you?"

"Just to always remember that I'm an Ashley Hall graduate."

"Have you noticed any difference in how they dress at Georgetown and how you dress?"

"The students are much more casual. The girls wear fingernail polish and lipstick."

"Anything you want must be negotiated with Hartleigh, whether its makeup or clothing. Don't go to James. He'll never understand. Hartleigh's the one you must convince."

"And me?" asked Dory.

"Oh," Susan said with a warm smile, "you're so attractive that you're going to have to beat off boys with a stick. Just make sure you don't allow them to have any of your money."

Susan stepped to the curb, put her fingers in her mouth, and whistled a cab to a stop.

Both girls gaped. They'd seen boys do this, but never a girl.

So an apartment was found and also a furniture dealer who handled repossessed furniture.

"Never pay full price," advised Susan. "There's going to be a lot of used furniture available during this depression."

After signing a lease on an apartment near Capitol

Hill, they returned to the Mayflower where, much to their surprise, Errol Fiske and Luke Andersen waited for them in the lobby. In a flash, everything Susan Moultrie had drilled into them about money and its relationship to independence was replaced by an entirely different set of expectations.

TWENTY-FOUR

Hartleigh hosted the young gentlemen in her sitting room—which the girls soon learned was the only place the boys would be allowed on the seventh floor.

"Actually," said Luke, "that's a problem. We don't have enough money for a hotel. We thought we could stay with you."

"Or at the YMCA," suggested Errol.

"Are you telling me you left Chicago without any money? Then how did you get here?"

"Well," said Luke, turning out his pockets and revealing a few coins, "we rode the rails."

Errol perked up. "Do you know how many people ride the rails these days, Mrs. Stuart?"

Dory became even more head over heels. Her boyfriend was doing just as he wished. Oh, to be a boy—or the girl he loved.

"We must let them stay here," injected Tessa.

"These boys need to talk with my husband," said Hartleigh. "He'll determine what's best."

"But Uncle James is out of town," complained Tessa.

"Then we'll wait for his return."

"But," asked Dory, "where will they stay?"

Hartleigh rose to her feet. Everyone else did, too.

"Wait here." She disappeared into her bedroom, returning with a dollar. "Here!" She thrust the bill toward Luke Andersen. "Escort the girls downstairs to the restaurant, and immediately after your meal return to the seventh floor."

The young people's faces lit up.

"Don't get ahead of yourselves. Both girls know the rules."

"Oh." Errol grinned. "Ashley Hall rules, right?"

"Then you also know my girls are going nowhere but that restaurant off the lobby. Understand?"

"Yes, ma'am," said the four teenagers, and out the door and into the elevator they trooped. Through the open door Hartleigh saw Milo shake his head and smile.

Once they left, Hartleigh placed a phone call to Charleston. The boys' visit made her stomach churn. Oh, why wasn't James here instead of flying around investigating some project for Jim Byrnes? There was absolutely no way to contact him until he called in tonight to speak with the children.

In Charleston, Christian Andersen was stunned to learn his younger brother was in Washington. He wanted to speak with him.

Hartleigh was ready for that. The teenagers had just reported back from their meal downstairs and were dancing to "Ah, But Is It Love?" on the radio in the sitting room.

Hartleigh held out the phone. "It's for you."

Luke pointed at his chest. "Me?" Who could possibly know he was in Washington?

Hartleigh sent the girls to their room and made Errol sit and wait his turn. From the smirk on Errol's face, Hartleigh believed the young man to have a flask of liquid courage on his hip. Errol's smirk disappeared when Christian asked for Errol's parents' phone number.

"There are no parents," said the young man, rising to his feet. "My grandmother raised me."

"Give me that number," said Christian over the phone. "If you won't listen to me, perhaps you'll listen to your grandmother."

"No, no, no!" pleaded Errol. "Don't do that! It'll break her heart. Please don't."

"Then you agree to leave Washington and return to your studies?" asked Christian.

"Yes, sir, whatever you say."

"Just make sure you take my brother along."

After the boys left, Hartleigh threw up in the toilet and reapplied a little makeup before going to the girls' room.

That's when all hell broke loose.

"You have no right to do this!" shouted Tessa.

Dory was sitting on the foot of the bed crying. Once again the rug had been jerked from under her. Maybe she didn't deserve true happiness.

"How in the world can you gang up on Luke like that?" demanded Tessa.

"Christian wants his brother to get an education."

"That doesn't mean we can't be together."

Hartleigh shook her head, Dory sobbed, and Tessa turned her back on her.

"I reject all of this," said Tessa, shoulders stiff. "I don't want any of this. I want to be with Luke."

"Tessa, it's important to marry well and to look past the rosy glow of hugs and kisses and ask what you and Luke have in common." Hartleigh reached for her ward's shoulder. "Tessa—"

The girl whirled around, and Hartleigh drew back.

"I won't hear it. You can't send away the man I love. You have James. It's only right I have Luke."

"But I didn't marry until I had a beau who could support me and my babies."

"I could help. Luke only has two years left at the university."

"In this economy, where will you find a job? Businesses don't hire women, they hire heads of households."

"I'll go to Uncle James. He's always helped me in the past."

"He's helped you out of a few childish scrapes, but why do you think he'd help you start your life in such a foolish manner?"

"My father will give me the money."

"He'll have to. More money won't be forthcoming from James. I forbid it."

Tessa glanced at Dory. No help there. Dory sat on the edge of the bed and stared at the floor. Tears ran down her cheeks.

"You didn't trust me to have a phone in this room," said Tessa, gesturing at the nightstand. "That's how much you care."

"You haven't seen Luke lately and absence makes the heart grow fonder."

"Don't quote platitudes to me. If I'd had more time with Luke in Chicago, you'd understand."

Hartleigh held her hands out, palms up. "James made it possible for you to spend nearly two weeks in Chicago. He's bent over backwards to help you be together though Christian's family doesn't want this match. Not now, they don't."

"The Andersens took in Rachel and Christian when Rachel's family wouldn't have them."

"The Andersens are good Christians, but they don't have the money to support another family, especially one living in Chicago and attending the university. It's your and Luke's obligation to do what's right. James and I've treated you fairly, and my mother's done right by Dory."

The runaway wiped away her tears and looked up from the bed. "Tessa, listen to Hartleigh. She knows what's best."

"But don't you see . . . ."

Dory shook her head and cut her eyes at Hartleigh.

Tessa nodded, then joined her friend on the end of the bed, downcast and resigned to their fate.

"Perhaps Luke can come to Charleston for the summer," suggested Hartleigh.

When Dory looked up, Hartleigh added, "Errol, too." She smiled. "James can find them jobs. Didn't James find a job for your brother when he moved to town? He works in the warehouse now, doesn't he?"

The girls said nothing and both of them moved rather mechanically preparing for bed. Hartleigh remained with them while they dressed, performed their toilet, and climbed into bed. She, however, wasn't there when the girls pulled the boys' clothing from under their beds, packed an overnight bag, and took the stairs to the ground floor. There a friendly bellhop called a taxi and sent them hurtling toward their future. And the girls did not fail to take along their bright, new shiny checkbooks.

When James and Lewis returned from Muscle Shoals, James found his wife demanding that he sic the Pinkertons on Dory and Tessa. It took a few minutes to make sense of what had happened, and Hartleigh would not calm down until James promised to fly to Chicago and return both girls to Washington.

"Once I get those girls back to Charleston, everything will work out." And Hartleigh left to be sick in the toilet again.

While Hartleigh was out of the room, the elevator doors opened and Dory's brother stepped off.

"What are you doing here?" asked James. Last time he'd seen the young man he had been working in the warehouse and sleeping on one of the bunk beds.

"Christian put me on a sleeper last night." He glanced up and down the hallway. "Where's Dory?"

James explained.

The young man set his jaw. "What are we doing about it?"

"Follow me." James went down the hall to Katie's room.

"Yes?" said the pilot as she opened the door.

"Pull yourself together. You have one more trip to make before you go to work for the *Piedmont*. We leave for Chicago in the morning. With any luck, we'll be there before anyone else."

While showing Dory's brother where to bunk for the night, James gestured at the nightstand. "They'll give you a wake-up call. Check the menu if you want something to eat." He glanced at his wristwatch. "The restaurant's closed, but the kitchen will send up sandwiches. I'll take a corned beef on rye."

"Corned beef? What's that?"

"Yankee foodstuff. Tastes pretty good with Russian dressing."

In the hallway, Lewis Belle returned from storing away his luggage. "Are you going to need me to remain in Washington?"

James shook his head. "Now that we've seen the potential for TVA, you should return to South Carolina and work with Strom Thurmond for the Santee-Cooper."

"My family has already left, but before I go, I'll report to Byrnes. Regarding the Santee-Cooper, my suspicion is that Charleston's mayor, Burnet Maybank, may be most receptive. Maybank understands that the Santee-Cooper could revolutionize life for those living in the Pee Dee."

Two days later, James and Katie returned to the seventh floor where James walked into his suite, put down his bag, and let out a long sigh. He knocked on his wife's door and upon entering her bedroom, he said, "They're married."

Hartleigh shrieked, doubled over, and couldn't stop shaking. Katie heard the screams and hustled down the hall and into the bedroom.

"Everything all right in here?"

"She didn't take the news very well." James sat on the bed with Hartleigh leaning into him. "I've sent for the doctor."

"Anything I can do?"

James shook his head.

Katie cleared her throat.

"What now?" he asked rather irritably.

"I've been thinking that with Dory in Chicago, I'll share that apartment with Susan Moultrie, if that's all right with you."

"It's fine." Where in the world did these people get the idea they had to run everything by him?

The following morning his wife, still in bed and with arms folded across her chest, said, "We'll get the marriages annulled."

"Both girls are eighteen." James took a seat on the side of her bed. "They get to make their own mistakes now."

Absentmindedly, Hartleigh picked at his sleeve. "But what will people think? What will my mother think? I was responsible for those girls."

"And they eloped."

Hartleigh let go of his shirt. "We should've never left Charleston." She straightened up against the pillows and headboard. "None of my children will ever set foot out of Charleston, I can promise you that."

"Dory's brother remained in Chicago. Perhaps there's hope."

Though James had no idea what that hope might be. The two girls had been found working at the world's fair where Dory draped herself across the new Cadillac V-16, the talk of the fair, while Tessa took up tickets from those who wished to see Sally Rand perform her infamous fan dance. While James and Tessa argued in the ticket booth, Rand was arrested for indecent exposure.

There was a tapping at the bedroom door, and the nanny came in holding the hands of the twins. "Sorry, ma'am, but they miss Tessa and Dory and I can't calm them."

Hartleigh thumped the bed with both hands. "You children climb in bed with me."

The twins screamed with excitement and clambered into the bed to snuggle under the covers.

Mary Anne looked up at her mother. "Will Tessa and Dory come home?"

"Why shouldn't they? Tessa and Dory love Charleston, and that's where we'll wait for them."

With that, James left the bedroom with the nanny.

"Is there anything else I can do, Captain Stuart?"

"I don't think so. My wife's mind is pretty much made up."

"To return to Charleston?"

"Actually to be reunited with her mother."

Two days later, James had the whole floor to himself, and as he stood in the empty hallway trying to make sense of the last few days, the elevator doors opened and Whitney stepped out.

"Oh, there you are, sir." With a suitcase in one hand and a walking stick in the other, the Wharton School graduate asked, "Where do we begin?"

James looked past the young man to the far end of the hallway and then stared in the opposite direction. "Well, whatever we do, it won't begin here."

After a long ride in Bernard Baruch's private railway car where Hartleigh had babysitters and plenty of time to consider her future, she and the twins disembarked in Charleston. On the platform Rachel Andersen and her mother waited.

The twins raced over and flung their arms around their grandmother's legs. Elizabeth bent down, hugged the children, and kissed them on top of their heads. She and Hartleigh embraced, but Rachel hung back. Behind Rachel stood a porter with a luggage cart.

"What's this about the Charleston Hotel?" asked her mother. "You have a beautiful home on South Battery and you're staying in a hotel? What will people think?"

"No, Mother, I have a beautiful home on South Battery but chose to reside in a hotel—what will people think of *you.*"

And Hartleigh shepherded the twins around her mother, handed her chit to the porter, and joined Rachel Andersen. The two young women embraced, then, already in animated conversation, strolled to Rachel's car in the parking lot.

ABOUT THE AUTHOR

Steve Brown is the author of the Belle family saga, which begins when Catherine and Nelie Belle arrive in Charles Towne just in time for Nelie to be kidnapped by Blackbeard and carried off to the Outer Banks. One hundred-fifty years later, and before the outbreak of the Civil War, the sixth generation of the family owns a huge rice plantation up the Cooper River; Franklin Belles goes off to West Point, his brother, Lewis, to the Citadel. Fifty years following that, three old maids, the great, great grandchildren of Catherine, take in an orphan, a victim of the moonshine feuds in the Carolina foothills. Fifteen years later, the Belle family is part of the Charleston scene during the Roaring Twenties; a year later, the effects of the Panic of 1929 hit those living south of Broad, followed by, in 1930, the rise of South Carolina Senator James Byrnes. And during the Sixties, Ginny Belle, thirteen-generation Charlestonian, spends her summers on Pawleys Island where she and her friends go to meet boys and dance.

The Pirate and the Belle
The Belles of Charleston
The Old Maids' Club
Charleston's Lonely Heart Hotel
Charleston's House of Stuart
Charleston on the Potomac
Carolina Girls

Bibliography

All in One Lifetime
James F. Byrnes

America 1933
Michael Golay

The Depression Years, 1933-1940
Anthony J. Badger

Eisenhower in War and Peace
Jean Edward Smith

Jim Farley's Story: The Roosevelt Years
James A. Farley

FDR
Jean Edward Smith

Franklin Delano Roosevelt
Alan Brinkley

Franklin Delano Roosevelt
Conrad Black

Greenville
The History of the City and County in the South Carolina
Piedmont
Archie Vernon Huff, Jr.

A New Deal
Stuart Chase

New Deal or Raw Deal?
How FDR's Economic Legacy Has Damaged America
Burton Folsom, Jr.

No Ordinary Time
Doris Kearns Goodwin

Nothing to Fear
Adam Cohen

The Palmetto State
The Making of Modern South Carolina
Jack Bass and W. Scott Poole

Sly and Able: A Political Biography of James F. Byrnes
David Robertson

CPSIA information can be obtained
at www.ICGtesting.com
Printed in the USA
FFOW04n0707291114
9044FF

CPSIA information can be obtained
at www.ICGtesting.com
Printed in the USA
BVHW03s1743180218
508446BV00001B/14/P